EX LIBRIS

EVERYMAN'S LIBRARY

EVERYMAN,
I WILL GO WITH THEE,
AND BE THY GUIDE,
IN THY MOST NEED
TO GO BY THY SIDE

ALBERT CAMUS

THE
OUTSIDER

TRANSLATED FROM THE FRENCH
BY JOSEPH LAREDO

WITH AN INTRODUCTION
BY PETER DUNWOODIE

EVERYMAN'S LIBRARY

139

First published in French as *L'Etranger* in 1942
This translation first published in Great Britain by Hamish Hamilton
in 1982
This translation copyright © Joseph Laredo, 1982
Published by arrangement with Hamish Hamilton Ltd.

The translator and publisher wish to thank Appleton-Century-Crofts
Incorporated for the use of the Afterword by Albert Camus which
originally appeared as the Preface to the American University
Edition of *The Outsider.*

First included in Everyman's Library, 1998
Introduction, Bibliography and Chronology © Everyman's Library,
1998
Typography by Peter B. Willberg

www.everymanslibrary.co.uk

ISBN: 978-1-85715-139-8

A CIP catalogue record for this book is available from the
British Library

Published by Everyman's Library,
50 Albemarle Street, London W1S 4DB

Distributed by Penguin Random House (UK) Ltd.,
20 Vauxhall Bridge Road, London SW1V 2SA

Printed and bound in Germany by GGP Media GmbH, Pössneck

THE OUTSIDER

CONTENTS

Introduction ix

Select Bibliography xxvi

Chronology xxviii

THE OUTSIDER

Part One I

Part Two 57

Afterword 115

INTRODUCTION

When *The Outsider* was published in occupied Paris in June 1942 the name Albert Camus meant nothing to the French public, for only a few hundred copies of the young writer's previous work (*The Right Side and the Wrong Side*, 1937; *Nuptials*, 1939) had been published and distributed in Algiers by the small-scale – though locally influential – publisher Edmond Charlot. By 1945 Camus was being ranked, along with Jean-Paul Sartre, as one of the foremost writers of the period and, to judge by recent estimates, which suggest that in French *The Outsider* has 200,000 new readers a year, it is clear that his reputation has not waned since then.

The impact of *The Outsider* was clearly paramount in forging Camus' reputation, but in the forties there were other reasons too, including fashion, circumstance and philosophy. Literature, cinema and the stage have given us all, whether those who lived through World War II or the post-war generations, images of life in occupied France. While commercial considerations help explain the preference given to the (often stereotyped) heroics of the Resistance, there is also a bleaker counterpart which depicts the vicissitudes of occupied France, the drudgery and dullness of everyday life for the majority in the daily struggle to earn a wage, obtain food and fuel; the uneasy coexistence of defeated, disheartened French and overbearing, often heavy-handed Germans; the insidious fear generated by identity checks, house searches and arbitrary arrests or deportation; the sullenness and uncertainty of the man-in-the-street, largely powerless once caught up in the system. This world of defeat and débâcle, anguish and ambiguity – but also, bravery and defiance – dominates the literature of the period, from the first novel of the forties to make an impact as specifically 'resistance literature', Vercors' *Le Silence de la mer* (1942), via Saint-Exupéry's *Pilote de guerre* (1942) to many of the Editions de Minuit's clandestine publications (Elsa Triolet's *Les Amants d'Avignon*, 1943, Claude Aveline's *Le Temps mort*, 1944, for instance). While the German

Propaganda-Abteilung saw no reason to censor *The Outsider* when it was submitted to them for approval under the terms of an agreement signed with all publishers still active during the Occupation (the chief adviser, Gerhard Heller, was in fact enthusiastic about it), the earliest readers of *The Outsider* recognized the bleak, claustrophobic world portrayed in Camus' novel. The bleakness, the banality and the sense of imprisonment were interpreted as an acute and accurate evocation of the feeling of the period, and the satire of a tainted legal system in which the innocent are brutalized and wrongly condemned struck many as a caustic depiction of the devalorized Vichy regime.

But Camus' growing reputation was not based solely on the ephemeral correspondence between a public mood and a particularly evocative fictional universe, for by 1945 he was also a well-known journalist. After completing his *licence* in philosophy and a diploma on Plotinus and St Augustine at the University of Algiers, Camus had had a number of jobs: clerk, salesman, teacher, technical assistant at the Algiers Meteorology Institute ... and, from 1938, reporter on the pro-Popular Front daily, *Alger républicain*. This trade-union-supported paper frequently attacked the actions and decisions of the political and economic establishment in Algeria, and it was in response to a particularly gross right-wing depiction of the beauty and delights of the famine-stricken Berber region of Kabylia that, in June 1939, the paper began publication of a major series of articles by Camus entitled 'Misère de la Kabylie', depicting the reality on the ground and demanding structural reform and the proper application of measures already voted. Given this type of outspoken attack on colonial policy in general and the Algerian government in particular, it was inevitable that, in the uncertain period leading up to the outbreak of war, *Alger républicain*'s line should lead to increasing conflict with the authorities. Once military censorship had been imposed, in July 1939, Camus and the paper's editor Pascal Pia embarked on a summer of skirmishes, tricks, protests and sundry subterfuges in order to make their voices heard. With the closure of *Alger républicain* in October of that year due to lack of newsprint, the two journalists transferred their campaign to its sister paper *Le Soir républicain* until, in January 1940, it was shut down in its turn, this time by decision of the Government-General. By August 1943 Pascal Pia had been assigned as editor to the underground newspaper *Combat*, organ of the clandestine Resistance movement of the same name (founded in 1942). By March 1944 Camus (who, by then, was working for one of the major Paris publishers, Gallimard) had himself begun writing for the paper. Like other Resistance newspapers such as *Défense de la France* and *Franc-Tireur*, it had a circulation of two to three hundred thousand. During the armed insurrection of August 1944, launched to liberate Paris, *Combat* published its first public issue under the stirring banner 'From Resistance to Revolution'. In the months that followed, Albert Camus' editorials were to become for thousands of Parisians the voice of a new generation, demanding retribution and renewal, in the name of justice and hope. Camus, journalist, novelist and playwright (*Le Malentendu*, 1944; *Caligula*, 1945), was firmly established on the Paris stage.

Fashion had its part to play too, however, for a companion piece to *The Outsider*, which Camus had hoped to publish simultaneously, brought him to the attention of Paris journalists anxious to popularize the rising philosophy of the period, Existentialism. While Camus always maintained that his essay *The Myth of Sisyphus* (1943) deals with the Absurd and is anti-Existentialist, surface similarities between *The Outsider*, the essay and the works of Jean-Paul Sartre, Simone de Beauvoir and others allowed journalists to place Camus squarely in the Existentialist camp, encouraged by the latter's friendship and close collaboration with Sartre's group. Indeed, *The Outsider*'s hero, Meursault, became for many *the* Existentialist hero, despite Camus' frequent protests, typified by this rather jocular statement on the confusion: 'No, I'm not an Existentialist. Sartre and I are always surprised to see our names linked. We are even thinking of publishing a little advertisement where the undersigned affirm that they have nothing in common and refuse to answer for each other's debts' (*Les Nouvelles littéraires*, 1945). The publication of *The Plague* (1947), which stresses solidarity and human values, was to scotch for the perspicacious reader any lingering confusion which had been generated largely by the historical and cultural context in which *The Outsider* was first published. While formally much less radical than Camus' first published novel, it was to reinforce his reputation as a major post-war writer.

*

The Outsider is a challenging work whose surface simplicity leads the reader through a series of largely mundane events towards an unresolvable ambiguity. The directness of the first-person narration in the first part, which reads like the hero's diary, is both enlightening and puzzling. Enlightening because the day-to-day events recounted have an immediacy and a directness or matter-of-factness which leave the reader with a sense of factual certainty. Yet puzzling, because the facts that Meursault has chosen to recount are frequently of less significance than those he has chosen to omit. Or rather, because the reader gradually becomes aware that what he has chosen to omit is not facts or events, but explanations. Faced with a surfeit of the one and a dearth of the other, the reader has to fall back on his or her own experience and values in order to probe the unsaid.

But it is precisely this process of interpretation which is satirized in Part II of the novel, once Meursault has been arrested for murder. The events with which we are by then familiar become the raw material not for the reconstruction of a sequence of events, but for the construction of a motive. The *fact* that Meursault killed an unnamed Arab on the beach is not in dispute; the issue is the *reason* for the killing, and in claiming to uncover that reason (whether it is called a sordid settling of accounts or simple self-defence) the lawyers resort to precisely the same technique as the reader of Part I. Both want to construct a causal chain from a number of apparently disconnected events; both claim to see inside the outsider.

*

If, on first contact with the novel, we let ourselves be guided by the title, then we might be inclined to see the hero, Meursault, as rather marginal, a misfit or an anti-social individual. Meursault, we discover, is a clerk and although he seems to be devoid of ambition (at least if this means leaving Algiers and moving to the company's Paris offices), there is no suggestion that his work is other than satisfactory. Indeed, his remarks show that he is very conscious of the demands of his boss as regards both time off and private telephone calls during office hours, and is keen to avoid trouble. Chapter 3 begins: 'I worked hard at the office today'; and chapter 4: 'I worked hard all week'. The firm's personnel department could certainly not accuse him of having an 'attitude problem'.

Similarly, this outsider has a perfectly normal circle of friends and acquaintances, some close, such as the local restaurateur Céleste, Meursault's colleague Emmanuel or his girlfriend Marie, others more casual, like his neighbours Salamano, to whom he offers comfort and advice when the latter loses his dog, and Raymond, for whom he writes the letter which, through a singularly haphazard sequence of events, will lead to Meursault's condemnation for murder. Indeed, as though to offset his own normality, he comments on behaviour which strikes him as amusing or odd: that of a 'peculiar ... robot-like' little woman who, while sharing his table, ticks off nearly every item in the week's radio programmes; the language habit of Raymond's friend Masson who concludes every statement by 'and what's more', even though, interjects Meursault somewhat sententiously, 'he didn't add anything to the meaning of his sentence'; the boisterous football supporters and, in particular, the cinema-goers still under the influence of the films they had just seen.

Although Camus himself stressed in the preface to an American edition in 1955 (printed in this edition as an Afterword), '[Meursault] is an outsider to the society in which he lives, wandering on the fringe, on the outskirts of life, solitary and sensual', his character's everyday behaviour and situation actually provide little evidence thereof. Indeed, when in Part II of the novel a lawyer attempts to label Meursault as different, anti-social, the response is quite explicit: 'I wanted to assure him that I was just like everyone else, exactly like everyone else.'

*

How then should we proceed in the face of this denial of difference? Can we, as readers, discover in the text factors which would allow us to see in Meursault an outsider? The answer will not be found in the judgments arrived at in Part II, where the bias of the legal procedures is highlighted not only in the hasty and uncorroborated conclusions drawn from such seemingly heinous acts as drinking white coffee at a mother's wake, not knowing her age or failing to shed tears during her funeral, but also in using such facts to condemn the accused as having 'no place in a society whose most fundamental rules [he] ignored'. The answer must be sought in Meursault's own statements and attitudes, and it is in these that we encounter the philosophy of the Absurd that Meursault embodies.

As Meursault and his new girlfriend Marie dress after going for a swim Marie notices his black tie and asks if he is in mourning: 'I told her that mother had died. She wanted to know when, so I said "Yesterday". She recoiled slightly, but made no remark.' A few days later, when asked if he wants to marry her: 'I said I didn't mind and we could do if she wanted to ... She then remarked that marriage was a serious matter. I said, "No". She didn't say anything for a moment and looked at me in silence ... After another moment's silence, she mumbled that I was peculiar, that that was probably why she loved me but that one day I might disgust her for the very same reason.' When asked by his defence counsel if his mother's death had upset him he replies: 'I probably loved mother quite a lot, but that didn't mean anything. To a certain extent all normal people sometimes wished their loved ones were dead. Here the lawyer interrupted me, looking very flustered.' Such responses are disconcerting not merely because they reveal the hero's rather brutal directness and honesty, but because these very qualities are used to *challenge* more normal conventions and values. As Camus put it, Meursault is condemned because 'he does not play the game', because, far from being the apparently indifferent unemotional individual that his account first suggests (where, like Marie, readers might indeed find him bizarre), his actions and statements are the direct consequence of a philosophical stance which rejects widespread social and moral norms. He is accused of indifference after putting his mother in a home or refusing to look at the corpse, yet he acknowledges that, once settled, she was happier with people of her own generation and, after her death, his first thought on reaching the old people's home is to see her body. He is accused of callousness because he smokes or drinks at her wake, yet he had thought about it beforehand and decided 'it really didn't matter'. Accused, in short, of not *displaying* conventional attitudes and reactions.

Meursault, then, is not an automaton, devoid of emotion, incapable of pleasure or reflection. On the contrary, it is in the name of alternative values that he undemonstratively opposes those of society. First and foremost among these values is, precisely, that of pleasure: whether in his work, on the beach, in his relations with Marie and his friends, even in prison, Meursault's primary concern is with immediate, sensual gratification. When such pleasures are unavailable, they can be dismissed; when offered, they are to be enjoyed; and from the outset the text makes it clear that the natural world (sky, sun, sea, light, warmth ...) is the primary source of such pleasure, to the extent that Marie, whether in the sea, on the sand or in the smell of salt left on her pillow, is essentially the embodiment of those natural elements. Meursault dismisses the (cultural) notion of love, but fully appreciates the force of desire.

Although the role of the sun is ambiguous – since it has a dehumanizing, destructive effect during the burial and the murder – it dominates the novel and provides the hero's moments of greatest intensity and feelings of happiness. Clearly, the influence of Camus' native Algeria is paramount in this valorization of the natural world, which is dominant in earlier Camus texts such as *The Right Side and the Wrong Side* and, more especially, the aptly named *Nuptials*. It is widely recognized as one of the essential ingredients in Camus' world view and it links him directly to the output of an earlier generation of writers, to the colonial novels of Louis Bertrand and the 'Algerianist' movement around Robert Randau, for whom the European-Algerian settler population was epitomized by physicality, raw energy and appetite. Camus' short essay 'Summer in Algiers' is a lyrical summary of the European's mythologizing self-perception and it provides a useful window on the French-Algerian world to which the hero of *The Outsider* belongs and which Camus characterized as excessive, offering no lessons for man but always ready 'to give, bountifully'. It is an arena reserved for the passions of youth, offered naked to the sun, and 'in this abundance and profusion, life adopts the movement of great passions, sudden, demanding, generous. It is not to be built, but to be consumed.' This perspective (which has been called neo-pagan), while turning its back on North Africa's Islamic cultural heritage, also spurned the more sophisticated and, according to Camus, 'cerebral' response to the Mediterranean in the work of writers like Valéry or Gide. Instead, Camus valorizes a race 'indifferent to spirituality (which) adores and admires the body'.

If Meursault became one of the most influential fictional figures of the post-war years, indeed one of those rare characters who acquire the status of myth and infiltrate the wider cultural scene, it is largely as a result of this rejection of conventional attitudes in the name of immediacy, spontaneity and the intensity of sense experience. As Camus' American preface asserted, Meursault is 'in love with a sun which leaves no shadows. Far from lacking all sensibility, he is driven by a tenacious and therefore profound passion, the passion for an absolute and for truth.' His defence of that truth, his absorption in the *hic et nunc*, is Camus' embodiment of the values that *The Myth of Sisyphus* proposes: individual life and happiness in a world of sensation and natural beauty; lucidity regarding man's mortality and the inanity of beliefs and responses designed to screen the reality thereof. Philosophically, it is at this level that Meursault is an outsider: not merely to society or convention, but to a world which is simultaneously the source of the Absurd man's happiness, and his anguish. For he knows, at the moment of greatest intensity or harmony, that he will one day be deprived of it all or that, as Caligula puts it in the play of 1945, 'men die and are not happy'. And this is precisely the argument with which Meursault, in a highly untypical outburst, counters the complacent assertions of the prison chaplain: 'He seemed so certain about everything, didn't he? And yet none of his certainties was worth one hair of a woman's head. He couldn't even be sure he was alive because he was living like a dead man. I might seem to be empty-handed. But I was sure of myself, sure of everything, surer than he was, sure of my life and sure of the death that was coming to me ... Nothing, nothing mattered and I knew very well why. He too knew why ... The others too would be condemned one day. He too would be condemned.'

It is on such statements that Jean-Paul Sartre probably based his assertion that 'although [Camus] owes something to Kierkegaard, Jaspers and Heidegger, his true masters are the French moralists of the seventeenth century. He is a classical Mediterranean ... The philosophy of Camus is a philosophy of the Absurd, and for him the Absurd springs from the relation of man to the world, of his legitimate aspirations to the vanity and futility of human wishes. The conclusions which he draws from it are those of classical pessimism.'

*

While the hero's outburst is highly articulate it does not provide an adequate explanation, and while Camus once suggested that 'if you want to be a philosopher, write novels', it is actually in *The Myth of Sisyphus* that one encounters the rational basis of Meursault's instinctive stance. Camus claimed that this essay, the novel and the two plays of the forties are expressions of the same philosophy and belong to a 'cycle of the Absurd', and they do effectively share a persuasive evocation of the absurdity of the human condition that French readers had already encountered in the work of Sartre, André Malraux or Kafka for instance.

Camus' essay is in harmony with Part I of *The Outsider* insofar as the Absurd is shown to be not the conclusion of a reflexive process but the awareness brought about by direct experience. And, like Meursault's existence prior to the murder, these experiences are resolutely banal: the routine, mechanical nature of everyday life, work and human action (see the descriptions as Meursault spends Sunday on his balcony); the 'meaningless pantomime' of social ritual (such as a wake or funeral); the empty words used to label human experience (such as 'love' or 'guilt'); a life in which each man's destiny is merely to age and die (like the old people of the home); the feeling that, at times, one is a stranger not merely for others but for oneself (as Meursault discovers when he catches sight of his reflection in a tin plate). But one day, on a street corner, on a beach, in a prison cell, 'you ask yourself why ...' and, suddenly awakened from a life of habit, the individual is brought face to face with the meaninglessness of existence, with the knowledge that nothing he/she does or does not do will change anything or prevent the inevitable. Now lucid, man sees himself caught up in a mechanism as inescapable, as perfectly adjusted, as efficient as the guillotine: 'what was wrong with the guillotine was that you had no chance at all, absolutely none. In fact it had been decided once and for all that the patient would die. It was a classified fact, a firmly fixed arrangement, a definite agreement which there was no question of going back on.' Man becomes conscious of being a prisoner condemned to death and, like Meursault who for a time clings desperately to the possibility of a successful appeal against his sentence, he may be tempted to cling to religion, philosophy or hope in an attempt to hide the truth about the 'bloody mathematics' of the human condition. Consequently, in his desire to unmask the truth, Camus in *The Myth of Sisyphus* discusses and repudiates not only the beliefs of Christianity but the reasoning of philosophers such as Kierkegaard, Chestov, Jaspers and Husserl, and the fictional solutions proposed by Kafka or Dostoevsky, names which were at the forefront of the debates raging in France in the thirties and forties.

The influence of Nietzsche is undeniable in this essay in which lucidity means recognizing the inanity of such palliatives and the concreteness of the only truth in man's possession, namely his individual existence in the here and now. It is in enjoying life to the full in the present, in living an ethic of quantity instead of quality, conscious that one day soon it will be too late, that the Absurd man reasserts his freedom and his innocence. And *The Myth of Sisyphus* proposes four illustrations of such a response: Don Juan who, in his conquests, gives primacy to sensation and multiplicity, rejecting notions like salvation/damnation (and love) as mere fiction; the actor who, in every role he plays, lives out with intensity a destiny whose order is an illusion and whose end is a foregone conclusion; the conqueror who, aware of the impermanence of conquest, is motivated solely by the pleasure of the quest; and finally, the creative artist, whose stubborn creations, unable to change the world, echo the lucidity and ultimate futility of the Absurd man's rebellion. While Camus' hero clearly lacks the energy evinced by such models, the end of the novel shows that he shares their passion; and it is precisely this mix of lethargy and intensity which struck a chord with an entire generation of writers and film-makers.

This is the philosophical position that underpins *The Outsider*, where Part I shows us an individual living out spontaneously, pre-reflexively, an Absurdist attitude to life, while Part II displays both his growing awareness and the mechanisms applied to marginalize him as an individual who has 'no place in a society whose most fundamental rules [he] ignored'.

I have suggested that Part II can be read as an attempt by the representatives of the legal system (both prosecution and defence) to forge a rational, causal sequence from the disconnected, random events which make up Meursault's existence in Part I in order to explain the killing of the unnamed Arab. Similarly, the chaplain's intervention in the last chapter of the novel can be interpreted as an attempt to merge legal guilt and moral responsibility, crime and sin. But Meursault does not know the meaning of the word 'sin', and has great difficulty in coming to terms with the fact that he is 'guilty', not because he does not understand the concepts, but because he has rejected the fundamental value systems on which they are based. If Meursault strikes (indeed disturbs) observers as indifferent and amoral, it is not because he is a detached, unemotional outsider, but because he is living and responding within a radically different scheme of values, one in which the past (regret) and the future (hope) are meaningless. Meursault is the embodiment of an *alternative* system which undermines the very basis of the judgment/condemnation to which he is subjected. At this stage in Camus' thinking (which *La Peste* was soon to obfuscate), in a world devoid of meaning no action has any more significance than any other action. Whether one kills or not, whether one marries or not, whether one is executed or not ... such things are not a matter of indifference but of 'equivalence', and it is this radical challenge to established values that the prosecutor rejects as an 'abyss threatening to swallow up society'. With *Caligula* Camus takes this philosophical stance to its logical conclusion in a striking portrayal of twentieth-century nihilism and in *La Peste*, unable to defeat the philosophy, he espouses a new humanism in an attempt to keep the monster in check.

*

But the success of *The Outsider* was (and is) not due solely to the depiction of this Absurdist philosophy, however influential that may have been; for the novel is also a major formal achievement which has had a lasting influence on post-war literature.

The two most salient features of the novel, perceived in the very first sentences, are the presence of a first-person narrator and the use of the perfect tense (lost, of course, in English, but highly unusual in French where the past historic is the normal literary tense). And it is this non-literary tense which serves as a signal from the outset that literary conventions – and, consequently, the reader's expectations – are to be flouted.

Prominent among such expectations, when faced with a first-person narrative, is the traditional pact between narrator and reader, inherited from eighteenth- and nineteenth-century fiction, the confidence not only that the text being read allows one to follow inner feelings and reactions but that the account itself is sincere. The traditional omniscient narrator may already have suffered many an indignity by 1942, but at least one could still count on a narrator either knowing all about himself or, as we find in the *récits* of André Gide for example, being narcissistically fascinated by his own emotions, ideas and development! Here, however, even if we were to shoehorn Meursault into this category, he fails signally to impart that knowledge to the reader since his account systematically eschews explanation and, while it is rich in concrete description, generates only uncertainty or oblique assessment. We learn less about Meursault than we would traditionally have gleaned from the account of a third-person narrator, and he maintains his opacity throughout the episodic, disjointed, highly individualized, day-to-day entries of Part I. Once the reader has encountered the artificial, inflated and conflicting explanations concocted in Part II, he/she may well be inclined to conclude that the search for an explanation is a vain pursuit. And such a conclusion would be in keeping with the Absurdist philosophical approach for which rational and mythical explanations are merely grand narratives invented to enrobe – and thus disguise – the disjointed, contingent reality of lived experience.

But Part II does not merely corroborate the narrative (and, perhaps, existential) choices that Meursault seems to have made when setting down his account of events; it also introduces an unexpected disruption in the narrative. Instead of the concreteness, the apparent spontaneity and the valorization of sensory information which dominate Part I and project an image of a carefree individual living unproblematically on the surface of experience (that he normally selects and controls as he pleases), Part II inserts the hero into a system dominated by causality and introspection, a system in which he is controlled and manipulated. Memory (for the narrator) and speculation (on the part of the lawyers) take over as the earlier account is reordered with hindsight and reassessed from within another value system. The narrator has become the outsider, at the centre of attention yet simultaneously alienated and dispossessed.

The contrast between the two parts is underlined by the language itself. Jean-Paul Sartre and Roland Barthes produced two of the earliest and most fruitful analyses of *The Outsider* in which, in an attempt to highlight the novelty of the flat, neutral, inert language used, they stressed the restricted, concrete, colourless and slightly monotonous qualities. For this non-literary language Barthes coined the expression the 'degree zero of writing', and in drawing attention to the links between the techniques and the philosophy underpinning them Sartre (in an article in February 1943) highlighted the discontinuity of a writing where sentences are merely juxta-posed or provided with minimal linkages such as 'but', 'then', 'and'. 'Each sentence of *The Outsider* is an island,' concluded Sartre in his description of this parataxis, closed in upon itself, cut off from the next by a void, and we tumble from sentence to sentence, from void to void, as the narrator aligns events but abstains from comment.

Later critics produced more extensive analyses of the novel's stylistic features, triggered primarily by the exceptional weight of metaphor in the closing pages of both Part I (the murder scene) and Part II which had been played down by both Sartre and Barthes in their attempts to account for the overall impression generated by the text. They concluded for instance that while the novel is actually far from devoid of literary characteristics (images, metaphors, lyrical description etc.), these are 'neutralized' by the colourless, a-literary language; or that the dominant impression is less that of a literary language embedded in a non-literary language than a cons-tant, carefully contrived slippage from one to the other.

*

Such debates may well seem somewhat arcane, but they have at least one advantage for us when we read a novel as intricate and as perplexing as *The Outsider*: they help to make us aware of some of the paths we, as readers, can explore. And it is precisely the noticeable change of style and focus in the second part of the novel which signals a shift in the narrator's objectives or, more precisely, which draws our attention to the question of objective. For while we might not normally ask ourselves *when* he wrote this account or, indeed *why* he did so, the change makes us aware of the fact that, as a narrator, he shifts from an immediate involvement with the people and events described in Part I (to the extent, for instance, of describing how he followed 'the little robot woman', or quot-ing at length from Raymond's account of his rather sordid affairs) to the position of observer and commentator in Part II. The motive behind the shift is Camus' desire to satirize the legal system, not merely in itself, but as representative of a society based on – indeed imposing – moral and social values which the Absurd man rejects. And satire requires distance.

This distance is achieved in Part II by a combination of two techniques. The first is a well-known technique exploited by writers as diverse as Voltaire, Montesquieu, Balzac, Stendhal, Flaubert and Céline, namely the use of the *ingénu* or naive observer who, by describing what he does not understand, renders the conventional unfamiliar and disrupts the automatic, routine enactment of words and gestures which have become transparent through repetition. 'It all seemed like a game,' asserts Meursault in the early days of his imprisonment, and once the trial gets under way he notes frequent failures on his part to understand, follow or appreciate events in the courtroom.

The second technique is based on the distance thus generated, as Meursault becomes increasingly aware that he is 'superfluous', 'useless', that everything is unfolding without him, that he is alienated from his own experiences. The legal system, with its clearly delineated roles and strictly hierarchical structure, is portrayed in theatrical terms in which the histrionic behaviour of the prosecuting judge, the inflated rhetoric of counsel, indeed the need for the journalists to write up the case to amuse their readers during the summer slump, all combine to drive home the image of a self-sufficient machine which, 'in the name of the French people', dehumanizes, marginalizes or destroys the individual and, in so doing, reinforces the Absurd. The court, in this Kafkaesque satire, is thus the voice of the value system of which the guillotine is the instrument, and Meursault the victim.

*

The reader's response to *The Outsider*, however, is rarely unambiguous or definitive, largely as a result of the uneasiness generated by the conflict between the beguiling surface simplicity of the language and its apparent colloquial directness on the one hand and, on the other hand, the avowed reluctance to speak of certain things and the deliberate refusal to explain such key issues as the time lapse between the first shot and the subsequent shots fired. 'But this time I didn't answer ...

Once again I didn't know what to answer … I still didn't say anything': if, as Camus once argued, Meursault is a hero 'who accepts to die for the truth', he is not a narrator who unfailingly tells the (whole) truth.

The Outsider demands to be re-read: overtly because Part II pushes one back to Part I in the search for confirmation or contradiction, covertly because it is a tantalizing display of the unsaid. Although the hero has frequently been interpreted as insensitive, for instance, the text bears several discreet traces of his emotional ties to his mother, from the 'Mother died today' of the opening sentence to the acknowledgement that 'For the first time in a very long time I thought of mother' of the last page, thus suggesting a possible avenue to the reader who wishes to tease out the understanding that the hero has reached. What, for example, is one to make of these two exceptional anecdotes, embedded in what is otherwise a rather terse text: the first a faded newspaper clipping about a son killed by his mother and sister; the second a story told by Meursault's mother, 'perhaps the only thing [he] really knew about [his father]', namely his decision to assist at the execution of a murderer and the nausea he had suffered as a result. And what is the meaning of Meursault's enigmatic conclusion: 'now I understood'?

Similarly, the reader's reaction to the apparent spontaneity of the account is disturbed by its unusual mix of skill, reticence and failure. Meursault displays the former as a writer in the letter written for Raymond and in the text written for the reader. Yet his reticence, as already suggested, is apparent in both the spoken word (in his unwillingness or inability to answer/explain) and the written word (in his display of directness, masking a refusal to elucidate). As for his failure, this can be traced throughout his communication with others: in the regret that he had not left certain things unsaid; in the defective exchanges on the beach; in the silence which surrounds the Europeans' encounters with the Arabs and which the former perceive as a provocation. Finally, it is gunshots that shatter that silence, replacing the unspoken word by a gesture interpreted later as aggression. It is this event which Meursault's own carefully constructed story will leave unexplained, and it is this absence of explanation which allows the court to manipulate the event and create a pretext on which he is condemned. Thus, by highlighting society's misunderstanding and foregrounding its involvement (and guilt) he shifts the reader's attention away from what he has himself left unsaid/unwritten.

*

'For the final consummation and for me to feel less lonely, I had only to wish that there be a large crowd of spectators the day of my execution and that they greet me with cries of hatred': this is merely the last of the many enigmas generated in *The Outsider* and it is one of the great merits of the present translation to have avoided the temptation of paraphrase and elucidation, rendering instead as closely as possible the precise phrasing of Camus' original, and thus enabling readers to appreciate why this stoical anti-hero and devious narrator remains one of the key expressions of a post-war Western *malaise*, and one of the cleverest exponents of a literature of ambiguity.

Peter Dunwoodie

SELECT BIBLIOGRAPHY

The most up-to-date biography is the very informative *Albert Camus, A Life* by Olivier Todd, Chatto & Windus, 1997.

The extensive critical interest that Camus' work attracts makes bibliography a daunting task, and the essential reference remains the outstanding work done by Robert F. Roeming since 1960. His *Camus: A Bibliography* is available on microfiche from the Camus Bibliography Research Collection, University of Wisconsin-Milwaukee.

The standard French edition of *The Outsider* appears in volume one of Camus' *Oeuvres complètes*, Bibliothèque de la Pléiade, Gallimard, Paris, 1962, edited by Roger Quilliot who is also the author of *La Mer et les prisons. Essai sur Albert Camus*, Gallimard NRF, Paris, revised edition, 1970 (English translation: *The Sea and Prisons: A Commentary on the life and thought of Albert Camus*, University of Alabama Press, Alabama, 1970). English translations, besides the one published here, include Stuart Gilbert's original translation for Hamish Hamilton, London, 1946, with an introduction by Cyril Connolly, and Matthew Ward's 1988 translation published by Alfred A. Knopf in the United States as *The Stranger*.

General critical studies of Camus' work abound, both in English and in French. Among the best-known early English ones, are that of Camus' ardent admirer Germaine Brée, *Camus*, Rutgers University Press, New Brunswick, 1959, and John Cruickshank's *Albert Camus and the Literature of Revolt*, Oxford University Press, London, 1959 (reprinted 1978). Both books provide a useful introduction. Other general studies include Philip Thody's straightforward *Albert Camus*, Macmillan, London, 1989; P. H. Rhein's *Albert Camus*, Twayne (TWAS), Boston, 1989; and *The Unique creation of Albert Camus*, Yale University Press, New Haven and London, 1973, written by Donald Lazere for an American public.

Monographs on specific aspects of the work are even more plentiful. E. Parker's *Albert Camus: The Artist in the arena*, University of Wisconsin Press, Madison, 1965, provides for instance a traditional, favourable view of Camus' ideological position and political commitment, countered by Conor Cruise O'Brien in a re-evaluation which stresses Camus' colonial conditioning, *Albert Camus of Europe and Africa*, Viking, New York, 1970. Jean Onimus produced a tendentious interpretation of an essentially Christian Camus, *Camus: face au mystère*, Desclée de Brouwer, Brussels, 1965; and R. Champigny a rather more convincing reading based on *The Outsider, Sur un héros païen*, Gallimard, Paris, 1959. My own *Writing French Algeria*, Oxford University Press, Oxford, 1998, includes chapters which situate Camus within the European-Algerian writing on/in the former French colony.

The Outsider has attracted a great deal of critical attention, of course, and Rosemarie Jones' *Camus: L'Etranger and La Chute*, volume 2 of the readily available Grant & Cutler series 'Critical Guides to French Texts', London, 1980, is an exceptionally lucid introduction to both novels. Four other texts provide remarkable insights into this many-faceted work: 'Explication de *l'Etranger*' in *Situations* I, Gallimard, Paris, 1947, where Jean-Paul Sartre applies *The Myth of Sisyphus* as a grid for his analysis; Roland Barthes, *Writing degree zero* (translated by A. Lavers and C. Smith, Cape, London, 1984), who uses Camus' text as a stick with which to beat the 'traditional' novel; B. T. Fitch's very complete overview, *L'Etranger d'Albert Camus. Un texte, ses lecteurs, leurs lectures: Etude méthodologique*, Larousse, Collection 'L', Paris, 1972; and finally, a Marxist reading of the language of *The Outsider* by Renée Balibar, *Les Français fictifs*, 1974.

Finally, for readers curious about the Paris of the forties and early fifties, three books can be recommended: the revealing though biased *Un Allemand à Paris 1940–1944* by the German Propaganda-Staffel officer Gerhard Heller, Seuil, 1981; Herbert Lottman's *The Left Bank: writers, artists and politics from the Front Populaire to the Cold War*, Heinemann, London, 1982; and a more specialized study of literature in occupied France by Margaret Atack, *Literature and the French Resistance. Cultural politics and narrative forms, 1940–1950*, Manchester University Press, Manchester and New York, 1989, which includes a very useful select bibliography.

CHRONOLOGY

DATE	AUTHOR'S LIFE	LITERARY CONTEXT
1913	Born in Mondovi, Algeria.	Proust: *Swann's Way*.
1914	Father mortally wounded at Battle of the Marne, awarded Croix de Guerre and Médaille Militaire. Trauma of his mother, Catherine Camus.	
1919		
1926		Hemingway: *The Sun Also Rises*. Malraux: *The Temptation of the West*.
1928		Gide: *The Counterfeiters*. Malraux: *The Conquerors*.
1929	Discovers the work of André Gide.	
1930	First attack of tuberculosis.	Malraux: *The Royal Way*.
1932	Articles in *Sud*.	Céline: *Journes to the End of the Night*.
1933	Student, University of Algiers.	Malraux: *Man's Fate*. J. Grenier: *Islands*. Faulkner: French trans. of *Sanctuary*.
1934	Marries Simone Hié. Job at the Algiers Préfecture as a clerk. First art reviews for *Alger-Etudiant*.	
1935	Joins Communist Party.	
1936	*Licence*. Starts theatre group. First play: adaptation of Malraux's *Days of Wrath*. Actor with Radio-Alger. Divorce.	Céline: *Death on the Instalment Plan*. Cain: French trans. of *The Postman Always Rings Twice*.
1937	Leaves Communist Party. *The Right Side and the Wrong Side*. Journalist: *Alger républicain*.	Caldwell: French trans. of *Tobacco Road*.
1938		Malraux: *Man's Hope*. Sartre: *Nausea*. Beckett: *Murphy*.
1939	Articles on Kabylia. *Nuptials*.	Sartre: *The Wall*. Steinbeck: French trans. of *Of Mice and Men*.

Outbreak of World War I.

Treaty of Versailles.

Centenary of the conquest of Algeria.

Hitler appointed Chancellor.

Anti-parliamentary riots by right-wing groups in an attempt to block the confidence vote for Daladier's Radical-Socialist government.

Abyssinia invaded. Franco-Soviet Pact. Malraux addresses the Algiers section of the Comité de Vigilance des Intellectuels Antifascistes. Popular Front government in France. Spanish Civil War.

Munich Agreement.

Germany invades Czechoslovakia. Spain falls to Franco. Germany invades Poland.

DATE	AUTHOR'S LIFE	LITERARY CONTEXT
1940	*Alger républicain* banned. Marries Françine Faure.	
1941	Returns to Oran. Finishes *Sisyphus*. The three absurds are now complete.	
1942	Convalescent in the Massif Central. *The Outsider*.	Ponge: *The Voice of Things*. Sartre: *The Flies*.
1943	Moves to Paris and works for Editions Gallimard. *The Myth of Sisyphus. Combat*.	Sartre: *Being and Nothingness*.
1944	*Cross Purpose*.	Sartre: *No Exit*.
1945	*Caligula. Letters to a German Friend*.	Sartre: *The Age of Reason*.
1947	Leaves *Combat. The Plague*.	
1948	*State of Siege*.	Sartre: *Dirty Hands* and *What is Literature?*
1949	*The Just*.	
1950	*Actuelles I*.	
1951	*The Rebel*. 'First series: Absurd ... Second series: Revolt.'	Death of André Gide.
1952		Quarrel with Sartre and the Surrealists. Beckett: *Waiting for Godot*.
1953	*Actuelles II*.	Barthes: *Writing Degree Zero*. Robbe-Grillet: *The Erasers*.
1954	*Summer*.	
1955	Writes for *L'Express*.	
1956	Separation from wife. Leaves *L'Express. The Fall*.	Sarraute: *The Age of Suspicion*. Céline: *Castle to Castle*.
1957	*Exile and the Kingdom*. Nobel Prize for Literature.	Robbe-Grillet: *Jealousy*. Beckett: *Endgame*.
1958	Brings together articles on Algeria: *Actuelles III. The Right Side and the Wrong Side* republished with preface.	Beckett: *Krapp's Last Tape*.
1959	Adaptation of Dostoevsky's *The Possessed*.	
1960	Killed in car crash at Villeblevin, 4 January. Unfinished novel: *Le Premier homme*.	

CHRONOLOGY

HISTORICAL EVENTS

Germany invades France. Assemblée Nationale votes full powers to Pétain.

Germany invades the Soviet Union.

Allied invasion of North Africa. The southern French 'Free Zone' occupied by the Germans. Comité National des Ecrivans set up to promote intellectual resistance.
Italy surrenders.

Allied landings in Normandy. Liberation of Paris.
Armistice.

Massacre in Sétif, Algeria. Rebellion against French rule in Madagascar.

Outbreak of the Algerian War of Independence.

Franco-British invasion of Suez. Budapest uprising.

OAS action in Algeria. General de Gaulle returns to power. Fifth Republic founded.

PART ONE

I

Mother died today. Or maybe yesterday, I don't know. I had a telegram from the home: 'Mother passed away. Funeral tomorrow. Yours sincerely.' That doesn't mean anything. It may have been yesterday.

The old people's home is at Marengo, fifty miles from Algiers. I'll catch the two o'clock bus and get there in the afternoon. Then I can keep the vigil and I'll come back tomorrow night. I asked my boss for two days off and he couldn't refuse under the circumstances. But he didn't seem pleased. I even said, 'It's not my fault.' He didn't answer. Then I thought maybe I shouldn't have said that. After all, it wasn't for me to apologize. It was more up to him to offer me his condolences. But he probably will do the day after tomorrow, when he sees me in mourning. For the moment it's almost as if mother were still alive. After the funeral though, the death will be a classified fact and the whole thing will have assumed a more official aura.

I caught the two o'clock bus. It was very hot. I ate at Céleste's restaurant, as usual. They all felt very sorry for me and Céleste told me, 'There's no one like a mother.' When I left, they came to the door with me. I was in a bit of a daze because I had to go up to Emmanuel's place to borrow a black tie and armband. He lost his uncle, a few months ago.

I had to run for the bus. It was probably all this dashing about and then the jolting and the smell of petrol and the glare of the sky reflecting off the road that made me doze off. I slept almost all the way. And when I woke up, I found myself cramped up against a soldier who smiled at me and asked me if I'd come far. I said, 'Yes' so as not to have to talk any more.

The home is just over a mile from the village. I walked it. I wanted to see mother straight away. But the caretaker told me I had to meet the warden. He was busy, so I waited a bit. The caretaker talked the whole time and then he showed me into the warden's office. He was a small, elderly man with the Legion of Honour. He looked at me with his bright eyes. Then he shook my hand and held it for so long that I didn't quite know how to take it back again. He consulted a file and told me, 'Mrs Meursault came here three years ago. You were her only means of support.' I felt as if he was reproaching me for something and I started to explain. But he interrupted me. 'You've no need to justify yourself, my dear boy. I've read your mother's file. You weren't able to look after her properly. She needed a nurse. You only have a modest income. And all things considered, she was happier here.' I said, 'Yes, sir.' He added, 'You see, she had friends here, people of her own age. She could share her interests with them. You're a young man, a different generation, and she must have been bored living with you.'

It was true. When she was at home, mother used to spend all her time just watching me in silence. She cried a lot the first few days at the old people's home. But that was only because she wasn't used to it. After a month or two she'd have cried if she'd been taken out of the home. Because by then she was used to it. That's partly why during this last year I hardly ever went to see her any more. And also because it meant giving up my Sunday – let alone making the effort of going to the bus stop, buying tickets and spending two hours travelling.

The warden spoke to me again. But I wasn't really listening any more. Then he said, 'I expect you'd like to see your mother.' I stood up without saying anything and he led the way to the door. On our way downstairs he explained, 'We've transferred her to our little mortuary. So as not to upset the others. Every time one of the inmates dies the others feel uneasy for two or three days. And that makes it difficult for the staff.' We crossed a courtyard where there were lots of old people, chatting in little groups. They'd stop talking as we went by, then behind us the conversations would start up again. It was like the muted chatter of budgerigars. At the door of a small building the warden stopped. 'I'll leave you now, Mr Meursault. If you need me for anything, I'll be in my office. We've arranged the funeral as usual for ten o'clock in the morning. We thought that that would enable you to watch over the departed tonight. One other thing: your mother apparently often mentioned to her friends that she wished to have a religious funeral. I've taken it upon myself to make the necessary arrangements. But I thought I should let you know.' I thanked him. Though she wasn't an atheist, mother had never given a thought to religion in her life.

I went in. It was a very bright room, with white-washed walls and a glass roof. The furniture consisted of some chairs and some cross-shaped trestles. Two of these, in the centre of the room, were supporting a coffin. The lid was on, but a row of shiny screws, which hadn't yet been tightened down, stood out against the walnut-stained wood. Near the coffin there was an Arab nurse in a white overall, with a brightly coloured scarf on her head.

At that point the caretaker came in behind me. He must have been running. He stuttered a bit. 'We covered her up. But I was to unscrew the coffin to let you see her.' He was just going up to the coffin when I stopped him. He said, 'Don't you want to?' I answered, 'No.' He didn't say anything and I was embarrassed because I felt I shouldn't have said that. After a moment he looked at me and asked, 'Why not?' but not reproachfully, just as if he wanted to know. I said, 'I don't know.' He began twiddling his white moustache and then, without looking at me, he announced, 'I understand.' He had beautiful bright blue eyes and a reddish complexion. He offered me a chair and then he sat down just behind me. The nurse stood up and went towards the door. At that point the caretaker said to me, 'It's a chancre she's got.' I didn't understand, so I looked at the nurse and saw that she had a bandage round her head just below the eyes. Where her nose should have been, the bandage was flat. Her face seemed to be nothing but a white bandage.

When she'd gone, the caretaker said, 'I'll leave you to yourself.' I must have made some sort of gesture, because he stayed where he was, standing right behind me. It made me feel uncomfortable having someone standing over me like that. The room was bathed in beautiful, late-afternoon sunshine. A couple of hornets were buzzing against the glass roof. And I was beginning to feel sleepy. Without turning round, I said to the caretaker, 'Have you been here long?' Straight away he answered, 'Five years' – as if he'd been waiting for me to ask all the time.

After that he chatted a lot. He'd have been very surprised if anyone had told him he'd end up as the caretaker of the Marengo home. He was sixty-four and he came from Paris. At that point I interrupted him, 'Oh, you're not from round here?' Then I remembered that before taking me to see the warden, he'd talked to me about mother. He'd told me that they had to get her buried quickly, because of the heat down in the plains, especially in this country. That was when he'd told me that he used to live in Paris and wouldn't easily forget it. In Paris they watch over the body for three or four days sometimes. But here you haven't even got time to get used to the idea before you have to start running after the hearse. Just then his wife had said to him, 'That's enough, that's not the sort of thing to be telling the gentleman.' The old man had blushed and apologized. I'd intervened to say, 'No. No.' He was right and I found what he was telling me interesting.

In the little mortuary he told me that he'd come to the home because he was destitute. He was in good health, so he'd offered to take on the job of caretaker. I pointed out to him that even so he was still an inmate. He said no. I'd already been struck by the way he referred to the inmates as 'they' or 'the others' or occasionally 'the old people', when some of them were no older than he was. But naturally, it wasn't the same thing. He was the caretaker, and to a certain extent he had authority over them.

The nurse came in at that point. Night had fallen suddenly. The sky had darkened rapidly above the glass roof. The caretaker turned the light-switch and I was blinded by the sudden blaze of light. He asked me if I wanted to go to the canteen to have some dinner. But I wasn't hungry. He then offered to bring me a cup of white coffee. I'm very fond of white coffee, so I accepted and he came back a few minutes later with a tray. I drank. I then wanted a cigarette. But I hesitated because I didn't know if I could smoke in front of mother. I thought it over, it really didn't matter. I offered the caretaker a cigarette and we smoked.

After a while, he said, 'You know, your mother's friends will be coming to watch over her too. It's the customary thing. I'll have to go and get some chairs and some black coffee.' I asked him if he could possibly turn off one of the lights. The glare from the white walls was tiring my eyes. He said he couldn't. That was how they'd been installed: it was all or nothing. I didn't pay much attention to him after that. He went in and out, arranging chairs. On one of them he stacked some cups round a coffee-pot. Then he sat down opposite me, on the other side of mother. The nurse was also on the far side of the room, with her back to me. I couldn't see what she was doing. But from the way her arms were moving, I assumed that she was knitting. It was nice, the coffee had warmed me up and through the open door I could smell flowers in the night air. I think I dozed off for a while.

It was a rustling sound that woke me. After having my eyes closed, the whiteness of the room seemed even more dazzling than before. There wasn't a shadow to be seen and every object, every angle and curve stood out so sharply that it was painful to the eyes. It was at that point that mother's friends came in. There were about ten of them in all, and they came gliding silently into the blinding light. They sat down without even a chair creaking. I saw them more clearly than I've ever seen anyone and not a single detail of either their faces or their clothes escaped me. And yet I couldn't hear them and I found it hard to believe that they really existed. Almost all the women were wearing aprons tied tightly round their waists, which made their swollen bellies stick out even more. I'd never noticed before what huge paunches old women can have. The men were almost all very thin and carrying walking-sticks. What struck me most about their faces was that I couldn't see their eyes, but only a faint glimmer among a nest of wrinkles. When they sat down most of them looked at me and nodded awkwardly, with their lips all sucked into their toothless mouths, and I couldn't tell whether they were greeting me or whether they just had a twitch. I think in fact they were greeting me. It was at that point that I realized they were all sitting opposite me round the caretaker, nodding their heads. For a moment I had the ridiculous impression that they were there to judge me.

Soon after that, one of the women started crying. She was in the second row, hidden behind one of her companions, and I couldn't see her very well. She was crying regularly, in little sobs: I thought she was never going to stop. The others didn't seem to notice. They sat slumped in their chairs, gloomy and silent, staring at the coffin or at their walking-sticks or at anything else, but without taking their eyes off it. The woman went on crying. I was very surprised because I didn't know who she was. I'd rather not have had to listen to her any more. But I didn't dare tell her. The caretaker leant over and spoke to her, but she shook her head, mumbled something and went on sobbing with the same regularity as before. The caretaker then moved round to my side and sat down next to me. He was silent for quite a long time. Then, without looking at me, he explained, 'She and your mother were very close. She says your mother was the only friend she had here and now she hasn't got anyone.'

We sat like this for quite some time. The woman began to sigh and sob less often. She sniffled for a while. Then at last she stopped. I didn't feel sleepy any more, but I was tired and my back was aching. Now it was all these people sitting in silence that was getting on my nerves. Except that every now and then I heard a strange noise and I couldn't understand what it was. In the end I realized that some of the old people were sucking at the insides of their mouths and letting out these peculiar clicking noises. They were so absorbed in their thoughts that they weren't aware they were doing it. I even had the impression that this dead body, lying there among them, didn't mean anything to them. But looking back I think it was the wrong impression.

The caretaker served us all some coffee. After that I don't know what happened. The night passed. I remember opening my eyes at one point and seeing all the old people slumped forward in sleep, except for one old man who had his chin resting on the back of his hands, which were clasped to his walking-stick, and who was staring at me intently as if he were just waiting for me to wake up. Then I slept some more. I woke up because the pain in my back was getting worse. The dawn was creeping up over the glass roof. Soon after that, one of the old men woke up and had a fit of coughing. He kept spitting into a large checked hand-kerchief and every time he did it it sounded as if his insides were being torn out. He woke up the others and the caretaker told them that they ought to be going. They stood up. This uncomfortable vigil had left them with ashen faces. On their way out, and to my great surprise, they all shook hands with me – as though a night spent in silence together had put us on intimate terms.

I was tired. The caretaker took me to his room and I was able to have a quick wash. I had some more white coffee which was very good. When I went outside, it was broad daylight. Above the hills which separate Marengo from the sea, the sky was full of red streaks. And the breeze coming up over the hills had a salty tang to it. It was going to be a beautiful day. It was a long time since I'd been out in the country and I knew how much I'd have enjoyed going for a walk if it hadn't been for mother.

But I waited in the courtyard, under a plane tree. I breathed in the fresh smells of the earth and I no longer felt sleepy. I thought of my colleagues at the office. At about this time they'd be getting up to go to work: for me it was always the most difficult time. I went on thinking like this for a bit, but I was distracted by the sound of a bell ringing inside the building. There was some commotion behind the windows, then everything calmed down again. The sun had risen a little higher in the sky: it was beginning to warm my feet up. The caretaker came across the courtyard and told me that the warden wanted to see me. I went to his office. He made me sign a number of documents. I noticed that he was dressed in black and wearing pin-striped trousers. He picked up the telephone and addressed me. 'The undertaker's men have just arrived. I'm going to ask them to close up the coffin. Before I do, would you like to see your mother one last time?' I said no. He gave the order into the telephone, lowering his voice, 'Figeac, tell the men they can go ahead.'

After that he told me that he would be attending the funeral and I thanked him. He sat down behind his desk and crossed his short legs. He informed me that he and I would be the only ones there, apart from the duty nurse. Usually the inmates weren't allowed to attend funerals. He only let them keep the vigil. 'It's kinder that way,' he remarked. But on this occasion he'd given an old friend of mother's, Thomas Pérez, permission to join the funeral procession. Here the warden smiled. He said, 'I know it's rather childish. But he and your mother were almost inseparable. Here at the home they used to tease them and tell Pérez, "She's your fiancée." He used to laugh. They enjoyed it. And the fact is that Mrs Meursault's death has affected him very badly. I didn't think I could refuse him permission. But on the advice of our visiting doctor, I forbade him to keep the vigil last night.'

We sat in silence for quite a long time. Then the

warden got up and looked out of the office window. After a while he remarked, 'Here comes the priest from Marengo. He's early.' He warned me that it would take at least three-quarters of an hour to walk to the church which is in the village itself. We went downstairs. In front of the little building stood the priest and two altar boys. One of them was holding a censer and the priest was bending over him to adjust the length of its silver chain. As we approached, the priest straightened up. He said a few words to me, addressing me as 'my son'. He went inside; I followed.

I noticed at once that the screws on the coffin had been tightened down and that there were four men in black in the room. At the same time I heard the warden telling me that the hearse was waiting in the road and the priest beginning his prayers. From that point on everything happened very quickly. The men moved towards the coffin with a pall. The priest, his followers, the warden and myself all went outside. By the door there was a woman I hadn't seen before. 'This is Mr Meursault,' the warden said. I didn't hear the woman's name, I just understood that she was the duty nurse. She bowed her head, without a trace of a smile on her long, bony face. We stood aside to make way for the body. Then we followed the pall bearers out of the home. Outside the gate stood the hearse. Bright, shiny and oblong, it looked a bit like a pencil box. Next to it stood the funeral director, a little man in a ridiculous outfit, and an old man who looked rather uncomfortable. I realized that this was Mr Pérez. He was wearing a soft felt hat with a round crown and a wide brim (he took it off when the coffin came through the gate), a suit with trousers that cork-screwed down onto his shoes and a black tie with a knot that was too small for the large white collar on his shirt. His lips were trembling beneath a nose pitted with blackheads. His thinnish white hair revealed curiously droopy, ragged ears whose blood-red colour made a striking contrast with the pallor of his face. The funeral director showed us to our places. The priest was to walk in front, followed by the hearse. On either side of the hearse, the four men. Behind it, the warden and myself and, bringing up the rear, the duty nurse and Mr Pérez.

The sun was already high in the sky. It was beginning to weigh down heavily on the earth and it was rapidly getting hotter. For some reason we waited quite a long time before setting off. I was hot under my dark clothes. The little old man, who'd put his hat back on, took it off again. I'd turned round slightly and was watching him when the warden started telling me about him. He told me that my mother and Mr Pérez often used to walk down to the village together in the evenings, accompanied by a nurse. I was looking at the country-side around me. Seeing the lines of cypresses leading away to the hills against the sky and the houses standing out here and there against the red and green earth, I understood mother. The evenings here must come as a kind of melancholy truce. But today, with the whole landscape flooded in sunshine and shimmering in the heat, it was inhospitable and depressing.

We set off. It was at that point that I noticed that Pérez had a slight limp. The hearse was gradually picking up speed and the old man was losing ground. One of the men round the hearse had also dropped back and was now walking level with me. I was surprised how rapidly the sun was climbing in the sky. I noticed that for quite some time now the countryside had been alive with the humming of insects and the crackling of grass. The sweat was running down my cheeks. I wasn't wearing a hat, so I fanned myself with my handkerchief. The man from the undertaker's then said something to me which I didn't hear. At the same time he was lifting the edge of his cap with his right hand and wiping his head with a handkerchief with his left. I said, 'Pardon?' He pointed up at the sky and repeated, 'Pretty hot.' I said, 'Yes.' A bit later, he asked, 'Is that your mother in there?' Again I said, 'Yes.' 'Was she old?' I answered, 'Fairly,' because I didn't know exactly. After that he didn't say any more. I turned round and saw old Pérez about fifty yards behind us. He was going as fast as he could, swinging his felt hat at arm's length. I also looked at the warden. He was walking in a very dignified way, without a single pointless movement. A few beads of sweat were forming on his brow, but he didn't wipe them off.

The procession seemed to be moving slightly faster. All around me there was still the same luminous, sun-drenched countryside. The glare from the sky was unbearable. At one point, we went over a section of road that had recently been resurfaced. The sun had burst open the tar. Our feet sank into it, leaving its shiny pulp exposed. Sticking up above the hearse, the coachman's boiled-leather hat looked as if it had been moulded out of the same black mud. I felt a bit lost, with the blue and white sky overhead and these monotonous colours all around me – the sticky black tar, the dull black clothes and the shiny black hearse. And what with the sun and the smell of leather and horse-dung from the hearse, and the smell of varnish and incense and the sleepless night I'd had, I was so tired that I could hardly see or think straight any more. I turned round again: Pérez seemed to be a long way away, lost in the heat-haze, then he disappeared altogether. I looked around and saw that he'd left the road and set off across country. I also noticed that there was a bend in the road ahead. I realized that Pérez, who knew the area, was taking a short cut in order to catch us up. By the time we were round the bend he was with us again. Then we lost him again. He cut across country once more and so it went on. All I could feel was the blood pounding in my temples.

After that everything happened so quickly and seemed so inevitable and natural that I don't remember any of it any more. Except for one thing: as we entered the village, the duty nurse spoke to me. She had a remarkable voice which didn't go with her face at all, a melodious, quavering voice. She said, 'If you go slowly, you risk getting sun-stroke. But if you go too fast, you perspire and then in the church you catch a chill.' She was right. There was no way out. I remember a few other scenes from that day as well: for instance, Pérez's face when he caught us up for the last time just outside the village. Great tears of frustration and anguish were streaming down his cheeks. But because of all the wrinkles, they didn't run off. They just spread out and ran together again, forming a watery glaze over his battered old face. Then there was the church and the villagers in the street, the red geraniums on the tombs in the cemetery, Pérez fainting (like a dislocated dummy), the blood-red earth tumbling onto mother's coffin, the white flesh of the roots mixed in with it, more people, voices, the village, the wait outside a café, the incessant drone of the engine, and my joy when the bus entered the nest of lights which was Algiers and I knew I was going to go to bed and sleep for a whole twelve hours.

2

When I woke up, I understood why my boss seemed unhappy when I asked him for my two days off: today's a Saturday. I'd sort of forgotten, but as I was getting up, it occurred to me. My boss, quite naturally, thought that I'd be getting four days' holiday including my Sunday and he couldn't have been very pleased about that. But for one thing, it isn't my fault if they buried mother yesterday instead of today and for another, I'd have had my Saturday and Sunday off in any case. Of course, I can still understand my boss's point of view.

I had trouble getting up because I was tired from the day before. While I was shaving, I wondered what to do with myself and I decided to go for a swim. I caught the tram down to the bathing station at the port. I dived straight into the narrows. It was full of young people. In the water I met Marie Cordona, who used to be a typist at the office. I'd fancied her at the time, and I think she fancied me too. But she left soon afterwards and nothing came of it. I helped her onto a buoy and as I did so, I brushed against her breasts. I was still in the water and she was already lying flat on her stomach on the buoy. She turned round towards me. She had her hair in her eyes and she was laughing. I hoisted myself onto the buoy beside her. It was good and as if for fun, I let my

head sink back onto her stomach. She didn't say anything and I left it there. I had the whole sky in my eyes
and it was all blue and gold. I could feel Marie's stomach
throbbing gently under the back of my neck. We lay on
the buoy for a long time, half asleep. When the sun got
too hot, she dived off and I followed. I caught her up,
put my arm round her waist and we swam together.
She was still laughing. On the quayside, while we were
drying ourselves, she said, 'I'm browner than you.'
I asked her if she wanted to come to the cinema that
evening. She laughed again and said there was a Fernandel film she'd like to see. When we'd got dressed again,
she seemed very surprised to see me in a black tie and
she asked me if I was in mourning. I told her that
mother had died. She wanted to know when, so I said,
'Yesterday.' She recoiled slightly, but made no remark.
I felt like telling her that it wasn't my fault, but I stopped
myself because I remembered that I'd already said that
to my boss. It didn't mean anything. In any case, you're
always partly to blame.

That evening Marie had forgotten all about it. The
film was funny in parts but otherwise really pretty
stupid. She had her leg against mine, and I was fondling
her breasts. Towards the end of the show I kissed her,
but badly. Afterwards she came back to my place.

When I woke up, Marie had gone. She'd explained
to me that she had to go and see her aunt. I remembered
that it was Sunday and that annoyed me: I don't like
Sundays. So I turned over in bed and tried to find the
salty smell of Marie's hair in the bolster and I slept till
ten. Then I stayed in bed and smoked a few cigarettes
till noon. I didn't want to have lunch at Céleste's as

usual because I knew they'd ask me questions and I don't like that. I cooked myself some eggs and ate them out of the pan, without any bread because I'd run out and I didn't feel like going down to buy some.

After lunch I was a bit bored and I wandered around the flat. It was just right when mother was here. But now it's too big for me and I've had to move the dining-room table into my bedroom. I live in just this one room now, with some rather saggy cane chairs, a wardrobe with a mirror that's gone yellow, a dressing-table and a brass bed. The rest is in a mess. A bit later, for want of something to do, I picked up an old newspaper and read it. I cut out an advertisement for Kruschen Salts and stuck it in an old exercise book where I put things that amuse me in the papers. I also washed my hands and finally went and sat out on the balcony.

My room looks out onto the main street of the sub-urb. It was a beautiful afternoon. And yet the pavements were grimy, and the few people that were about were all in a hurry. First of all it was families out for a walk, two little boys in sailor suits, with the trousers below their knees, looking a bit cramped in their stiff clothes, and a little girl with a big pink bow and black patent leather shoes. Behind them the mother, an enormous woman in a brown silk dress, and the father, a small, rather frail man whom I know by sight. He was wearing a straw hat and a bow tie and carrying a walking-stick. Seeing him with his wife, I understood why local people said he was distinguished. A bit later the local lads went by, hair greased back, red ties, tight-fitting jackets with embroidered handkerchiefs in their top pockets and square-toed shoes. I thought they must be heading for the cinemas in the town centre. That was why they were leaving so early and hurrying to catch a tram, laughing noisily as they went.

After that the street gradually became deserted. The shows had all started, I suppose. Only the shopkeepers and the cats remained. The sky was clear but dull above the fig-trees which line the street. The tobacconist opposite brought a chair out onto the pavement, placed it in front of his door and sat astride it, with his arms resting on the back. The trams, which had been cram-full a few minutes before, were now almost empty. In the little café Chez Pierrot, next door to the tobacco-nist's, the waiter was sweeping up the sawdust and the place was deserted. A typical Sunday.

I turned my chair round like the tobacconist's because I found it more comfortable that way. I smoked a couple of cigarettes, went inside to get some chocolate and came back to the window to eat it. Soon after that, the sky clouded over and I thought we were going to have a summer storm. It gradually cleared again though. But the passing clouds had left a sort of threat of rain hanging over the street which made it more gloomy. I watched the sky for a long time.

At five o'clock there was a lot of noise as some trams arrived. They were coming back from the local foot-ball-ground with bunches of spectators perched on the steps and hanging from the guardrails. The next few trams brought back the players; I recognized them by their little suitcases. They were yelling and singing at the tops of their voices that their team would never die. Several of them waved to me. One of them even shouted to me, 'We thrashed them.' I nodded, as if to say, 'Yes.' From that point on the street began to fill with cars.

The day advanced a bit more. Above the roofs the sky began to redden and with evening approaching, the streets came to life. People were gradually returning from their walks. I recognized the distinguished gentleman in the crowd. The children were either crying or trailing behind. Almost immediately, the local cinemas poured their audiences out in a great flood onto the street. The young men among them were making more decisive gestures than usual and I thought they must have seen an adventure film. Those who'd been to the cinemas in town came back a bit later. They looked more serious. They were still laughing, but only occasionally, and they seemed tired and thoughtful. They hung about in the street, wandering up and down the pavement opposite. The local girls, with their hair down, were walking arm in arm. The young men had positioned themselves so that the girls would pass by them and they'd throw out witty comments which would make the girls giggle and turn their heads away. I knew several of the girls and they waved to me.

The street lamps suddenly came on just then and they made the first few stars that were appearing in the night sky look quite pale. I could feel my eyes getting tired watching the street like this with its mass of people and lights. The street lamps were making reflections on the wet pavements, and the trams, passing at regular intervals, would light up a smile or some shiny hair or a silver bracelet. Soon afterwards, as the trams became fewer and the sky blackened above the trees and the lamps, the people gradually disappeared, until the street was deserted again and the first cat walked slowly across it. I thought maybe I ought to have some dinner. I had a bit of a neck-ache from leaning on the back of my chair for so long. I went down to buy some bread and some pasta, I did my cooking and I ate standing up. I wanted to smoke a cigarette at the window, but it had turned chilly and I felt a bit cold. So I closed my windows and as I was coming back inside I saw reflected in the mirror a corner of my table where my spirit-lamp was standing beside some pieces of bread. I realized that I'd managed to get through another Sunday, that mother was now buried, that I was going to go back to work and that, after all, nothing had changed.

3

I worked hard at the office today. My boss was kind. He asked me if I wasn't too tired and he also wanted to know how old mother was. I said, 'About sixty,' so as not to get it wrong and for some reason he seemed to be relieved and to regard the matter as closed.

There was a whole stack of bills of lading piling up on my desk and I had to go through them all. Before leaving the office to go for lunch, I washed my hands. I like doing this at lunchtime. I don't enjoy it so much in the evening because the roller towel which people use is all wet: it's been there all day. I mentioned this once to my boss. He replied that he found it regrettable, but that it was none the less a detail which didn't matter. I left a bit late, at half past twelve, with Emmanuel, who works in dispatch. The office overlooks the sea and we spent a few minutes just watching the boats in the harbour in the burning sunshine. At that point a lorry came rushing along with its chains rattling and its engine backfiring. Emmanuel said, 'Let's go,' and I started running. The lorry overtook us and we chased after it. I was swamped by the noise and the dust. I couldn't see a thing and all I was conscious of was the speed of this chaotic dash, in and out of cranes and winches, with masts dancing on the horizon and ships' hulls rushing by alongside. I caught hold first and took a flying leap. Then I helped Emmanuel up. We were both out of breath and the lorry was jumping about in the sun and the dust on the rough cobbles of the quayside. Emmanuel was laughing so much he could hardly breathe.

We arrived at Céleste's dripping with sweat. He was there as usual, with his paunch and his apron and his white moustache. He asked me if I was 'all right then'. I said yes and I was hungry. I ate very quickly and had some coffee. Then I went home and slept for a bit because I'd drunk too much wine and when I woke up, I felt like a cigarette. It was late and I ran to catch a tram. I worked all afternoon. It was very hot in the office and in the evening, when I left, I was glad to walk slowly back along by the docks. The sky was green and I felt happy. All the same, I went straight home because I wanted to cook myself some boiled potatoes.

On my way upstairs, in the dark, I bumped into old Salamano, my next-door neighbour. He had his dog with him. They've been together for eight years. The spaniel has got a skin disease – mange, I think – which makes almost all its hair fall out and covers it with brown blotches and scabs. After living with it for so long, the two of them alone together in one tiny room, Salamano has ended up looking like the dog. He's got reddish scabs on his face and his hair is thin and yellow. And the dog has developed something of its master's walk, all hunched up with its neck stretched forward and its nose sticking out. They look as if they belong to the same species and yet they hate each other. Twice a day, at eleven o'clock and six, the old man takes his dog for a walk. In eight years they haven't changed their route. You can see them in the rue de Lyon, the dog dragging the man along until old Salamano stumbles. Then he beats the dog and swears at it. The dog cringes in fear and trails behind. At that point it's the old man's turn to drag it along. When the dog forgets, it starts pulling its master along again and gets beaten and sworn at again. Then they both stop on the pavement and stare at each other, the dog in terror, the man in hatred. It's like that every day. When the dog wants to urinate, the old man won't give it time and drags it on, so that the spaniel scatters a trail of little drops behind it. But if the dog ever does it in the room, then it gets beaten again. It's been going on like that for eight years. Céleste always says, 'It's dreadful,' but in fact you can never tell. When I met him on the stairs, Salamano was busy swearing at his dog. He was saying, 'Filthy, lousy animal!' and the dog was whimpering. I said, 'Good evening,' but the old man went on swearing. So I asked him what the dog had done. He didn't answer. He just went on saying, 'Filthy, lousy animal!' I could just about see him, bent over his dog, busy fiddling with something on its collar. I asked again a bit louder. Then, without turning round, he answered with a sort of suppressed fury, 'He's always there.' Then he set off, dragging the animal after him as it trailed its feet along the ground, whimpering.

Just then my other next-door neighbour came in. Local people say he lives off women. When you ask him what he does though, he's a 'warehouseman'. Most people don't like him much. But he often talks to me and sometimes comes round for a minute or two because I listen to him. I find what he says interesting.

Besides, I've got no reason not to talk to him. He's called Raymond Sintès. He's fairly short, with broad shoulders and a nose like a boxer. He's always dressed very smartly. He also said to me once, when we were talking about Salamano, 'Isn't it dreadful!' He asked me if it didn't disgust me and I said no.

We went upstairs and I was about to say goodnight to him when he said, 'I've got some wine and black pudding in my room. Do you want to have a bite to eat with me? . . .' I realized that this would save me having to cook for myself and I accepted. He also only has one room, and a kitchen with no window. Above his bed there's a pink and white plaster angel, some photos of famous sportsmen and two or three pin-ups. The room was dirty and the bed unmade. First he lit his paraffin lamp and then he took a rather dubious-looking bandage out of his pocket and wrapped it round his right hand. I asked him what he'd done. He told me he'd had a fight with a bloke who was looking for trouble.

'You see, Meursault,' he said, 'it's not that I'm a troublemaker, but I'm no coward. This bloke, he said to me, "Get down off that tram, if you're a man." I said to him, "Just calm down, okay." Then he said I wasn't a man. So I got down and I said to him, "All right, that's enough, or you'll get flattened." He said, "Who by?" So I let him have it, and he went down. Me, I was going to help him up. But he started kicking me from off the ground. So I gave him one with my knee and a couple of swipes. His face was covered in blood. I asked him if he'd had enough. He said, "Yes." ' All this time, Sintès was fiddling with his bandage. I was sitting on the bed. He said, 'So you see it wasn't me who started it. He went for me first.' It was true and I agreed. Then be announced that in fact he wanted to ask my advice about this business, because I was a man of the world and I could help him and afterwards he'd be my mate. I didn't say anything and he asked me again if I wanted to be his mate. I said I didn't mind: he seemed pleased. He got out some black pudding, fried it up and put some glasses, plates, knives and forks and two bottles of wine on the table. All this in silence. Then we sat down. As we ate, he started telling me his story. He hesitated a bit at first. 'There was this girl ... she was sort of my mistress.' The man he'd had a fight with was this girl's brother. He told me that he'd been keeping her. I didn't say anything and yet he added immediately that he knew what local people said, but that he had a clear conscience and he was a warehouseman.

'To get back to my story,' he said, 'I realized that there was some deceiving going on.' He used to give her just enough to live on. He paid her rent for her and gave her twenty francs a day for food. 'Three hundred francs for the room, six hundred francs for food, a pair of stockings every now and then, that made it a thousand francs. Her ladyship didn't work. But she kept telling me that it wasn't enough, that she couldn't manage with what I was giving her. And yet I kept telling her, "Why don't you get a part-time job? You'd make things easier for me, with all these little extras. I bought you a new suit this month, I give you twenty francs a day, I pay your rent and you go and have coffee with your friends every afternoon. You provide the coffee and sugar. But I provide the money. I've been fair with you and now you're being unfair with me." But she wouldn't work, she just kept telling me that she couldn't manage and that's how I realized that there was some deceiving going on.'

He then told me that he'd found a lottery ticket in her bag and she hadn't been able to explain how she'd paid for it. A bit later he'd found 'a pawn-ticket' in her room which showed that she'd pawned two bracelets. Until then he hadn't even known these bracelets existed. 'I could tell that there was some deceiving going on. So I left her. But first I hit her. And then I told her a few home-truths. I told her that all she was interested in was putting it about. What I told her was this, you see, Meursault, "You don't realize that everyone's jealous of the happiness I give you. One day you'll know how happy you were."'

He'd beaten her till she'd bled. Before that he hadn't used to beat her. 'I used to hit her, but sort of affectionately. She'd yell a bit. I'd close the shutters and it'd finish the way it always does. But this time I really mean it. And I don't think I've punished her enough.'

He then explained that this was what he needed some advice about. He stopped to adjust the wick on the lamp which was charring. I was still listening. I'd drunk almost a litre of wine and my temples were burning. I was smoking Raymond's cigarettes because I'd run out. The last trams were passing and the few remaining street-noises fading away with them into the distance. Raymond went on. What annoyed him was that he 'still felt like sleeping with her'. But he wanted to punish her. First he'd thought of taking her to a hotel and calling in the vice squad to cause a scandal and have her registered as a prostitute. After that he'd gone to some friends he had in the underworld. They had no ideas. And as Raymond pointed out to me, so much for being in the underworld. That's what he'd told them and they'd then suggested 'marking' her. But that wasn't what he wanted. He'd think it over. First he wanted to ask me something. Then again, before he asked me, he wanted to know what I thought about this story. I told him that I hadn't thought about it but it was interesting. He asked me if I thought there was some deceiving going on, and as far as I could see, it did seem as if there was some deceiving going on, and if I thought she should be punished and what I'd do in his position, and I said you could never tell, but I understood why he should want to punish her. I drank a bit more wine. He lit a cigarette and told me his plan. He wanted to write her a letter 'which would really hurt and at the same time make her sorry'. Then, when she came back, he'd go to bed with her and 'right at the crucial moment' he'd spit in her face and throw her out. I agreed that that would punish her all right. But Raymond told me that he didn't feel capable of writing the kind of letter that was needed and that he'd thought I might draft it for him. When I didn't say anything, he asked me if I'd mind doing it right away and I said no.

He stood up after drinking another glass of wine. He pushed aside the plates and the bit of cold pudding that we'd left. He carefully wiped the oilcloth that was on the table. Then he took out of a drawer in his bedside table a sheet of squared paper, a yellow envelope, a small red wooden pen-box and a square inkpot with purple ink in it. When he told me the girl's name I realized she was Moorish. I wrote the letter. I did it rather haphazardly, but I did my best to please Raymond because I had no reason not to please him. Then I read it out. He listened, smoking and nodding his head, then he asked me to read it again. He was extremely pleased. He told me, 'I could tell you were a man of the world.' I didn't notice at first, but he was calling me by my first name. It was only when he announced, 'Now you're really my mate,' and used it again that it struck me. He repeated his remark and I said, 'Yes.' I didn't mind being his mate and he really seemed keen on it. He put the letter in the envelope and we finished off the wine. Then we sat and smoked for a while in silence. Outside, everything was quiet and we heard the swish of a passing car. I said, 'It's late.' Raymond agreed. He remarked on how quickly time passed, and in a way it was true. I felt sleepy, but it was too much trouble to get up. I must have looked tired because Raymond told me not to let go of myself. At first I didn't understand. Then he explained that he'd heard about mother's death but that it was something that was bound to happen sooner or later. That was what I thought too.

I got up. Raymond shook my hand warmly and said that we men always understood one another. I went out and, closing the door behind me, I paused for a moment in the dark, on the landing. The house was quiet and a vague breath of moist air was wafting up from the depths of the stair-well. All I could hear was the blood throbbing in my ears. I stood quite still. But in old Salamano's room, the dog whimpered feebly.

4

I worked hard all week and Raymond came and told me that he'd sent the letter. I went to the cinema a couple of times with Emmanuel who doesn't always understand what's going on. So you have to explain things to him. Yesterday was Saturday and Marie came over as we'd arranged. I really fancied her because she was wearing a pretty red and white striped dress and leather sandals. You could see the shape of her firm breasts and her suntanned face was like a flower. We caught a bus and went a few miles out of Algiers, to a little beach surrounded by rocks and bordered inland by reeds. The four o'clock sun wasn't too hot, but the water was warm and rippled with long, lazy waves. Marie taught me a game. You had to drink from the crest of the waves as you swam along, gathering all the foam in your mouth, and then turn on your back and spurt it up at the sky. This made a lacy spray which melted into the air or fell back in a warm shower onto my face. But after a while my mouth was burning with the bitterness of the salt. Then Marie joined me and clung to me in the water. She pressed her mouth to mine. Her tongue cooled my lips and we rolled in the waves for a while.

When we'd got dressed again on the beach, Marie looked at me with sparkling eyes. I kissed her. From that point on, neither of us said anything. I held her to me as we hurried to catch a bus, get back home and throw ourselves onto my bed. I'd left my window open and it was good to feel the summer night flowing over our brown bodies.

This morning Marie stayed and I told her that we could have lunch together. I went down to buy some meat. On my way back up I heard a woman's voice in Raymond's room. A bit later old Salamano swore at his dog; we heard the sound of footsteps and the scratching of paws on the wooden stairs and then, 'Filthy, lousy animal', and they went out into the street. I told Marie all about the old man and she laughed. She was wearing a pair of my pyjamas with the sleeves rolled up. When she laughed, I fancied her again. A minute later she asked me if I loved her. I told her that it didn't mean anything but that I didn't think so. She looked sad. But as we were getting lunch ready, and for no apparent reason, she laughed again, so I kissed her. It was at that point that we heard a row break out in Raymond's room.

First we heard a woman's shrill voice and then Raymond saying, 'You cheated on me, you cheated on me. I'll teach you to cheat on me.' Some dull thuds and the woman screamed, but it was such a terrifying scream that the landing immediately filled with people. Marie and I went out too. The woman went on yelling and Raymond went on hitting her. Marie said it was terrible and I didn't say anything. She asked me to go and fetch a policeman, but I told her that I didn't like policemen. Anyway, one came along with the plumber who lives on the second floor. He banged on the door and the noise stopped. He banged harder and after a moment the woman started crying and Raymond opened the door. He had a cigarette in his mouth and a sugary smile on his face. The girl rushed to the door and announced to the policeman that Raymond had hit her. 'Name?' the policeman said. Raymond told him. 'Take that cigarette out of your mouth when you're talking to me,' the policeman said. Raymond hesitated, looked at me and drew on his cigarette. At that the policeman hit him really hard with a thick, heavy slap, right across the cheek. The cigarette fell several yards away. Raymond's expression changed, but he didn't say anything for a moment and then in a humble voice he asked if he could pick up his fag. The policeman told him he could and added, 'But next time you'll remember not to clown around with policemen.' All this time the girl was crying and she repeated, 'He hit me. He's a pimp.' 'Excuse me, officer,' Raymond put in, 'isn't that against the law, that, calling a man a pimp?' But the policeman told him to 'shut his mouth'. Raymond then turned to the girl and said, 'Just you wait, my pet, we'll be seeing each other again.' The policeman told him to shut it and said that the girl was to go and he was to wait in his room until he was summoned to the police station. He added that Raymond ought to be ashamed of himself, being so drunk that he was shaking the way he was. At that Raymond explained, 'I'm not drunk, officer. It's just that I'm standing here, with you in front of me, and I'm shaking, I can't help it.' He closed his door and everyone went away. Marie and I finished getting lunch ready. But she wasn't hungry, I ate nearly all of it. She left at one and I slept for a bit.

At about three there was a knock on my door and Raymond came in. I didn't get up. He sat down on the edge of my bed. He didn't say anything for a minute and I asked him how it had gone. He told me that he'd done what he wanted to do but that she'd slapped him and so he'd beaten her up. I'd seen the rest. I told him I thought that this time she'd really been punished and he ought to be pleased. He agreed and pointed out that whatever the policeman did, he couldn't take back the blows she'd received. He added that he knew all about policemen and knew exactly how to handle them. He then asked me if I'd expected him to hit the policeman back. I replied that I didn't expect anything at all and anyway I didn't like policemen. Raymond seemed very pleased. He asked me if I'd like to go out for a walk with him. I got up and started combing my hair. He told me that I'd have to act as a witness for him. I said I didn't mind, only I didn't know what I was supposed to say. According to Raymond, all I had to do was to say that the girl had cheated on him. I agreed to act as a witness for him.

We went out and Raymond bought me a brandy. Then he wanted a game of billiards and I just lost. After that he wanted to go to a brothel, but I said no because I don't like that sort of thing. So we made our way slowly back and he kept telling me how pleased he was that he'd managed to punish his mistress. I found him very friendly towards me and I thought it was a good moment.

From some distance away I noticed old Salamano standing on the doorstep looking flustered. When we got nearer, I saw that his dog wasn't with him. He'd look in all directions, spin round, peer into the darkness of the hall, mumble a string of unconnected words and then start searching the street again with his little red eyes. When Raymond asked him what was wrong, he didn't answer at first. I vaguely heard him muttering, 'Filthy, lousy animal,' and he went on flustering. I asked him where his dog was. He replied abruptly that he'd disappeared. And then all of a sudden he spoke rapidly: 'I took him to the Parade Ground, as usual. There were crowds of people, round the stalls at the fair. I stopped to watch "the Escape King". And when I turned to go, he wasn't there any more. Of course, I'd been meaning to get him a smaller collar for a long time. But I never thought the lousy animal could disappear like that.'

Raymond then explained that the dog might just have got lost and that it would come back. He cited cases of dogs that had travelled dozens of miles to get back to their masters. This only seemed to make the old man more flustered. 'But they'll take him away from me, don't you see? If only someone would take him in. But they won't, everyone's disgusted by his scabs. The police'll get him, I know they will.' So I told him he should go to the pound and they'd give it back to him for a small charge. He asked me how much the charge was. I didn't know. Then he got angry: 'Pay money for that lousy animal. Ha! He can die for all I care!' And he started swearing at it. Raymond laughed and went inside the building. I followed him and we said good-night to each other on the upstairs landing. A minute later I heard the old man's footsteps and he knocked at my door. When I opened it, he stood for a moment in the doorway and said, 'Excuse me, excuse me.' I asked

him in, but he didn't want to. He was looking down at
his boots and his scabby hands were trembling. Without
looking up at me, he asked, 'They won't take him away
from me, will they, Mr Meursault. They will give him
back to me. Otherwise what will I do?' I told him that
they kept dogs at the pound for three days for their
owners to collect them and that after that they dealt
with them as they saw fit. He looked at me in silence.
Then he said, 'Goodnight.' He closed his door and
I heard him pacing up and down. Then his bed creaked.
And from the peculiar little noise coming through the
partition wall, I realized that he was crying. For some
reason I thought of mother. But I had to get up early in
the morning. I wasn't hungry and I went to bed without
any dinner.

5

Raymond phoned me at the office. He told me that a friend of his (he'd spoken to him about me) had invited me to spend the day next Sunday at his chalet, just out-side Algiers. I said I'd really like to, but I'd promised to spend the day with a girl-friend. Raymond immediately announced that she was invited too. His friend's wife would be only too pleased not to be the only woman among a crowd of men.

I wanted to hang up straight away because I know my boss doesn't like people ringing us up from town. But Raymond asked me to hold on and told me that he could have passed on this invitation that evening, but he wanted to warn me about something else. He'd been followed all day by a group of Arabs and one of them was the brother of his former mistress. 'If you see him near the house this evening when you come home, warn me.' I told him I would.

Soon after that, my boss sent for me and for a moment I was annoyed because I thought he was going to tell me to do a bit less phoning and a bit more work. But that wasn't it at all. He announced that he wanted to talk to me about a project he was vaguely considering. He just wanted to hear what I thought of the idea. He intended to set up an office in Paris to handle that side of the business on the spot by dealing directly with the big companies and he wanted to know if I was prepared to go over there. I'd be able to live in Paris and travel around for part of the year as well. 'You're a young man, and I imagine that sort of life must appeal to you.' I said yes but really I didn't mind. He then asked me if I wasn't interested in changing my life. I replied that you could never change your life, that in any case one life was as good as another and that I wasn't at all dissatisfied with mine here. He looked upset and told me that I always evaded the question and that I had no ambition, which was disastrous in the business world. So I went back to work. I'd rather not have upset him, but I couldn't see any reason for changing my life. Come to think of it, I wasn't unhappy. When I was a student, I had plenty of that sort of ambition. But when I had to give up my studies, I very soon realized that none of it really mattered.

That evening, Marie came round for me and asked me if I wanted to marry her. I said I didn't mind and we could do if she wanted to. She then wanted to know if I loved her. I replied as I had done once already, that it didn't mean anything but that I probably didn't. 'Why marry me then?' she said. I explained to her that it really didn't matter and that if she wanted to, we could get married. Anyway, she was the one who was asking me and I was simply saying yes. She then remarked that marriage was a serious matter. I said, 'No.' She didn't say anything for a moment and looked at me in silence. Then she spoke. She just wanted to know if I'd have accepted the same proposal if it had come from another woman, with whom I had a similar relationship. I said,

'Naturally.' She then said she wondered if she loved me and well, I had no idea about that. After another moment's silence, she mumbled that I was peculiar, that that was probably why she loved me but that one day I might disgust her for the very same reason. I didn't say anything, having nothing to add, so she smiled and took my arm and announced that she wanted to marry me. I replied that we'd do so whenever she liked. I then told her about my boss's proposal and Marie said she'd like to see Paris. I told her that I'd lived there once and she asked me what it was like. I said, 'It's dirty. Full of pigeons and dark courtyards. The people have all got white skin.'

Then we went for a walk across the town by its main streets. There were beautiful women everywhere and I asked Marie if she'd noticed. She said yes and she understood me. For a while neither of us said anything. I wanted her to stay with me though and I told her that we could have dinner together at Céleste's. She'd really have liked to but she was doing something. We were near my place and I said goodbye to her. She looked at me. 'Don't you want to know what I'm doing?' I did want to know, but I hadn't thought of asking and now she seemed to be reproaching me for it. Then, seeing me looking perplexed, she laughed again and bent her whole body towards me to give me a kiss.

I had dinner at Céleste's. I'd just started eating when a peculiar little woman came in and asked me if she could sit at my table. Naturally, she could. She moved in a series of jerks and her bright-eyed little face was like an apple. She took off her jacket, sat down and studied the menu feverishly. She called Céleste over and ordered her whole meal at once, speaking precisely but rapidly. While she was waiting for her hors d'oeuvre she opened her bag, took out a small square of paper and a pencil, added up the bill in advance, then took the exact sum, plus a tip, out of her waistcoat pocket and placed it in front of her. At that point the hors d'oeuvre arrived and she gulped it down as fast as she could. While she was waiting for the next course, she dived into her bag again and took out a blue pencil and a magazine which gave the radio programmes for the week. One by one, she very carefully ticked almost every programme. The magazine had a dozen or so pages, so this meticulous task occupied her throughout the meal. I'd already finished and she was still ticking away with the same diligence. Then she stood up, put her jacket back on with the same precise, robot-like movements and left. I didn't have anything to do, so I left as well and followed her for a bit. She'd taken up a position on the edge of the pavement and was making her way along with incredible speed and assurance without either changing course or looking round. I ended up losing sight of her and turned back. I thought how peculiar she was, but I fairly soon forgot about her.

Outside my door I found old Salamano. I asked him in and he told me that his dog was definitely lost, because it wasn't at the pound. The people there had told him that it might have been run over. He'd asked them if he could possibly find out at a police station. He'd been told that they didn't keep records of things like that, because they happened every day. I told old Salamano that he could get another dog, but he rightly pointed out to me that he'd got used to this one.

I was crouched on my bed and Salamano had sat down on a chair by the table. He was facing me, with both his hands on his knees. He still had his old felt hat on. He was mumbling half-finished sentences into his yellowing moustache. He was annoying me a bit, but I didn't have anything to do and I didn't feel sleepy. To make conversation, I asked him about his dog. He told me that he'd got it when his wife had died. He'd married fairly late. As a young man he'd wanted to go into the theatre: in the army he used to act in military vaudevilles. But he'd ended up working on the railways and he didn't regret it, because now he had a small pension. He hadn't been happy with his wife, but on the whole he'd got quite used to her. When she'd died he'd felt very lonely. So he'd asked a friend in the workshop for a dog and he'd got this one as a puppy. He'd had to feed it from a bottle. But since a dog doesn't live as long as a man, they'd ended up growing old together. 'He was bad-tempered,' Salamano said. 'Every now and then we had a right old row. But he was a nice dog all the same.' I said he was a good breed and Salamano looked pleased. 'Yes,' he added, 'but you should have seen him before his illness. His coat was his best point.' Every night and every morning, after it got that skin trouble, Salamano used to rub it with ointment. But according to him, its real trouble was old age, and there's no cure for old age.

At that point I yawned and the old man said he'd be going. I told him that he could stay, and that I was upset about what had happened to his dog: he thanked me. He told me that mother used to be very fond of his dog. He referred to her as 'your poor mother'. He seemed to assume that I'd been very unhappy ever since mother had died and I didn't say anything. Then, very quickly as if he was embarrassed, he told me that he realized that local people thought badly of me for sending my mother to a home, but that he knew me better and he knew I loved mother very much. I replied, I still don't know why, that I hadn't realized before that people thought badly of me for doing that, but that the home had seemed the natural thing since I didn't have enough money to have mother looked after. 'Anyway,' I added, 'she'd run out of things to say to me a long time ago and she'd got bored of being alone.' 'Yes,' he said, 'and at least in a home you can make a few friends.' Then he said he must go. He wanted to get some sleep. His life had changed now and he didn't quite know what he was going to do. For the first time since I'd known him, and with a rather secretive gesture, he gave me his hand and I felt the scales on his skin. He smiled slightly and before he went, he said, 'I hope the dogs don't bark tonight. I always think it's mine.'

6

That Sunday I had trouble waking up and Marie had to shout at me and shake me. We didn't eat anything because we wanted to be in the water early. I felt completely empty and I had a bit of a headache. My cigarette tasted bitter. Marie made fun of me because she said I had 'a face like a funeral'. She'd put on a white linen dress and let her hair down. I told her she was beautiful and she laughed with delight.

On our way down we knocked at Raymond's door. He told us he was just coming. Out in the street, because I was tired and also because we hadn't opened the shutters, the bright morning sunshine hit me like a slap in the face. Marie was jumping with joy and kept on saying what a beautiful day it was. I began to feel better and I noticed that I was hungry. I told Marie and she pointed to her oilcloth bag where she'd put our swimming costumes and a towel. I just had to wait and we heard Raymond shutting his door. He was wearing blue trousers and a white short-sleeved shirt. But he'd put a straw hat on, which made Marie laugh, and his forearms were all white under the black hairs. I was rather disgusted. He was whistling as he came down and he seemed really pleased. He said, 'Hi there, old man,' to me and addressed Marie as 'Miss'.

The day before, we'd been to the police station and I'd testified that the girl had 'cheated' on Raymond. He got off with a warning. They didn't check my statement. On the doorstep we talked about it with Raymond, and then we decided to catch the bus. The beach wasn't very far away, but we'd get there more quickly that way. Raymond said he thought his friend would be pleased to see us arrive early. We were just about to set off when Raymond suddenly pointed across the street. I looked and saw a group of Arabs leaning against the front of the tobacconist's shop. They were looking at us in silence, but in their own special way, as if we were nothing more than blocks of stone or dead trees. Raymond told me that the second one from the left was his man, and he looked worried. He added that anyway it was all settled now. Marie didn't really understand and asked us what was wrong. I told her that these Arabs had something against Raymond. She wanted to get going at once. Raymond straightened up and laughed, saying we'd better get a move on.

We went towards the bus stop which was a bit further along and Raymond informed me that the Arabs weren't following us. I looked round. They were still in the same place and looking with the same indifference at the spot where we'd just been. We caught the bus. Raymond, who seemed altogether relieved, kept on cracking jokes for Marie. I could tell that he liked her, but she hardly said a word to him. Every now and then she'd glance at him and laugh.

We went down into the suburbs of Algiers. The beach isn't far from the bus stop. But we had to cross a small plateau which overlooks the sea and then shelves down steeply to the beach. It was covered with yellow-ish rocks and brilliant white asphodels standing out against what was already a hard blue sky. Marie amused herself by swinging her oilcloth bag about and scatter-ing petals everywhere. We walked along between rows of little villas with green or white fences, some half-buried, with their verandas overgrown with tamarisk, others standing naked among the rocks. Before we reached the edge of the plateau, we could already see the motionless surface of the sea and, further along, a massive promontory drowsing in the clear water. The faint hum of an engine wafted towards us through the still air. And in the distance we saw a tiny trawler mov-ing imperceptibly across the dazzling sea. Marie picked some rock irises. From the slope leading down to the beach, we could see that there were already some people swimming.

Raymond's friend had a little wooden chalet at the far end of the beach. The house part backed onto some rocks while the piles supporting the front waded right into the water. Raymond introduced us. His friend was called Masson. He was a huge, broad-shouldered fellow, with a plump and friendly little wife, who had a Parisian accent. He immediately told us to make ourselves at home and said they'd fried us some fish which he'd caught that same morning. I told him how much I liked his house. He informed me that he spent his Saturdays and Sundays and all his holidays there. 'I get on well with my wife,' he added. And just then his wife was laughing with Marie. For the first time perhaps, I really thought I'd get married.

Masson wanted to go for a swim, but his wife and

Raymond didn't want to come. The three of us went down and Marie plunged straight into the water. Masson and I waited a bit. He spoke slowly and I noticed that he had a habit of finishing off every statement he made with an 'and what's more', even when, in fact, he didn't add anything to the meaning of his sentence. Referring to Marie, he said, 'She's stunning, and what's more, charming.' After that I didn't take any more notice of this habit of his because I was concentrating on feeling the sun doing me good. The sand was beginning to get hot underfoot. I denied myself the water for a bit longer, but I ended up saying to Masson, 'Let's go.' I dived in. He went in slowly and only took the plunge when he got out of his depth. He swam breast-stroke and rather badly too, so I left him behind and joined Marie. The water was cold and I was glad to be swimming. Marie and I swam right out, moving together and feeling content together.

Out in the open we lay on our backs and with my face turned towards the sky I could feel the sun peeling away the last few layers of water which trickled down into my mouth. We saw Masson making his way back to the beach to stretch out in the sun. From a distance he looked enormous. Marie wanted us to swim together. I went behind her to hold her round the waist and she swam with her arms while I helped by kicking with my feet. The little splashing sound followed us through the morning air until I began to feel tired. So then I left Marie and made my way back, swimming steadily and breathing regularly. On the beach I stretched out flat on my stomach beside Masson and put my face in the sand. I said it was good and he agreed. Soon afterwards Marie came up. I turned round to watch her coming. She was glistening all over with salty water and holding her hair back off her face. She lay down alongside me and the warmth of her body and the heat of the sun made me doze off a bit.

Marie shook me and told me that Masson had gone back up to the house, it was time for lunch. I got up straight away because I was hungry, but Marie told me that I hadn't kissed her all morning. It was true and yet I wanted to. 'Come into the water,' she said. We ran and sprawled in the little waves at the edge. We swam a few strokes and she clung on to me. I felt her legs round mine and I wanted her.

When we got back, Masson was already calling us. I said I was very hungry and he immediately announced to his wife that he liked me. The bread was good, and I devoured my share of the fish. After that there was some meat and fried potatoes. We all ate in silence. Masson drank a lot of wine and kept on filling my glass. By the time it came to the coffee, I had rather a thick head and I smoked a lot. Masson, Raymond and I thought of spending the whole of August together at the beach, sharing expenses. Suddenly Marie said, 'Do you know what time it is? It's half past eleven.' We were all surprised, but Masson said we'd eaten very early and that was quite natural because the time to have lunch was when you felt hungry. For some reason that made Marie laugh. I think she'd had a bit too much to drink. Masson then asked me if I wanted to go for a walk on the beach with him. 'My wife always has a siesta after lunch. But I don't like doing that. I have to go for a walk. I'm always telling her that it's better for the health. But after all, it's up to her.' Marie announced that she'd stay and help Mrs Masson with the washing-up. The little Parisian woman said that for that they'd have to get rid of the men. The three of us went out.

The sun was shining almost vertically onto the sand and the glare from the sea was unbearable. There was no one left on the beach. From the chalets running along the edge of the plateau and overlooking the sea came the sound of cutlery on crockery. It was hard to breathe in the dry heat rising from the ground. To begin with, Raymond and Masson discussed people and things I knew nothing about. I gathered that they'd known each other for some time and had even lived together once. We made our way down to the water and walked along the edge of the sea. Now and then a little wave would come up higher than the others and wet our canvas shoes. I wasn't thinking about anything because the sun beating down on my bare head was making me feel sleepy.

At that point Raymond said something to Masson which I didn't quite hear. But at the same time, right at the far end of the beach and a long way from where we were, I noticed two Arabs in boiler suits coming towards us. I looked at Raymond and he said, 'It's him.' We walked on. Masson wondered how they'd managed to follow us all this way. I thought they'd probably seen us getting on the bus with a beach-bag, but I didn't say anything.

The Arabs were advancing slowly and they were already much nearer. We didn't change pace, but Raymond said, 'If there's a fight, Masson, you take the one on the right. I'll take care of my man. Meursault, if another one turns up, he's yours.' I said, 'Yes' and Masson put his hands in his pockets. The sand was so hot that it seemed to have turned red. We were advancing steadily towards the Arabs. The distance between us diminished regularly. When we were within a few paces of each other, the Arabs stopped. Masson and I slowed down. Raymond went straight up to his man. I didn't quite hear what he said to him, but the Arab made as if to butt him with his head. Raymond then struck the first blow and immediately shouted to Masson. Masson went up to the one he'd been assigned to and hit him twice with all his strength. The Arab fell flat in the water, face down, and lay there for several seconds, with bubbles bursting on the surface, round his head. Meanwhile Raymond had hit the other one as well and his face was covered in blood. Raymond turned to me and said, 'You wait till I've finished with him.' I shouted, 'Look out, he's got a knife!' But already Raymond had his arm cut open and his mouth gashed.

Masson sprang forward. But the other Arab had got up again and he went round behind the one with the knife. We didn't dare move. They backed slowly away, without taking their eyes off us and keeping us at bay with the knife. When they thought they were at a safe distance, they ran off as fast as they could, and we were left pinned to the ground beneath the sun with Raymond clutching at his arm which was dripping with blood.

Masson immediately said that there was a doctor who spent his Sundays up on the plateau. Raymond wanted to go straight to him. But every time he spoke the blood from his wound bubbled up inside his mouth. We helped him back to the chalet as quickly as we could. When we got there, Raymond said that his wounds were only superficial and he could walk to the doctor's. He left with Masson and I stayed to explain to the women what had happened. Mrs Masson was in tears and Marie had gone very pale. It annoyed me to have to explain things to them. I ended up not saying anything and just smoked and watched the sea.

At about half past one Raymond came back with Masson. He had his arm bandaged up and some sticking-plaster on the corner of his mouth. The doctor had told him it was nothing, but Raymond looked very gloomy. Masson tried to make him laugh. But he still wouldn't speak. When he said that he was going down onto the beach, I asked him where he was going. He told me that he wanted to get some air. Masson and I said we'd go with him. At that he got angry and swore at us. Masson said we mustn't argue with him. But I followed him all the same.

We walked for a long time on the beach. The sun was crashing down onto the sea and the sand and shattering into little pieces. I had the impression that Raymond knew where he was going, but I was probably wrong. Right at the far end of the beach we came at last to a little spring, running down through the sand, behind a large rock. There we found our two Arabs. They were lying down, in their greasy boiler suits. They seemed quite calm and almost contented. Our arrival had no effect on them. The one who had attacked Raymond was watching him in silence. The other one was blow-ing down a small reed; watching us out of the corner of his eye, he was repeating over and over again the only three notes the instrument would make.

All this time there was just the sun and the silence, with the sound of the little spring and the three notes. Then Raymond put his hand to his hip-pocket, but the Arabs didn't move, they just kept looking at each other. I noticed that the one who was playing the flute had his toes spread right apart. But without taking his eyes off his adversary, Raymond asked me, 'Shall I let him have it?' I thought if I said no he'd get himself worked up and be bound to shoot. I simply told him, 'He hasn't said anything to you yet. It'd be unfair to shoot just like that.' Again there was the sound of the water and the flute amidst the silence and the heat. Then Raymond said, 'I'll insult him then, and when he answers back, I'll let him have it.' I answered, 'All right. But if he doesn't draw his knife, you can't shoot.' Raymond started getting a bit worked up. The other Arab was still playing and both of them were watching Raymond's every movement. 'No,' I said to Raymond, 'take him on hand to hand and give me your gun. If the other one intervenes, or if he draws his knife, I'll let him have it.'

When Raymond handed me his gun, the sun glinted off it. And yet still we remained motionless as if everything had closed in around us. We just stared fixedly at one another and here amid the sand, the sun and the sea, in the dual silence of the flute and the water, everything was at a standstill. I realized at that point that you could either shoot or not shoot. But suddenly the Arabs retreated and slid round behind the rock. So Raymond and I turned back. He seemed to be feeling better and talked about the bus home.

I went as far as the chalet with him but, while he climbed the wooden steps, I stayed at the bottom, with my head ringing from the sun, unable to face the effort of climbing the wooden staircase and having to confront the women again. But it was so hot that it was equally unbearable just standing there in the blinding rain that was pouring down out of the sky. Whether I stayed there or moved, it would come to the same thing. After a minute or two I turned back towards the beach and started walking.

There was still the same dazzling red glare. The little waves were lapping restlessly at the sand as the stifled sea gasped for breath. I was walking slowly towards the rocks and I could feel my forehead swelling up under the sun. The heat was pushing full against me as I tried to walk. And every time I felt the blast of its hot breath on my face, I set my teeth, closed my fists in my trouser pockets and tensed my whole body in defiance of the sun and of the drunken haze it was pouring into me. With every blade of light that leapt up off the sand, from a white shell or a piece of broken glass, my jaws tightened. I walked for a long time.

From a distance I could see the small, dark lump of rock surrounded by a blinding halo of light and spray. I was thinking of the cool spring behind the rock. I wanted to hear the murmur of its water again, to escape from the sun and the effort and the women's tears, and to relax in the shade again. But when I got nearer, I saw that Raymond's Arab had come back.

He was alone. He was lying on his back, with his hands behind his head, his forehead in the shade of the rock, and his whole body in the sun. His boiler suit was steaming in the heat. I was a bit surprised. As far as I was concerned, it was all settled and I'd gone there without even thinking about it.

As soon as he saw me, he sat up slightly and put his hand in his pocket. Naturally, I gripped Raymond's gun inside my jacket. Then he lay back again, but without taking his hand out of his pocket. I was some distance away from him, about ten yards or so. Every now and then I could see him looking at me, through half-closed eyes. But for most of the time he was just a shape dancing in front of me in the scorching air. The waves sounded even longer and lazier than they had been at midday. It was still the same sun, the same light and the same sand as before. For two hours now the day had stood still, for two hours it had been anchored in an ocean of molten metal. Out on the horizon a tiny steamer went by and I could just see it as a black speck out of the corner of my eye, because I hadn't stopped looking at the Arab.

I realized that I only had to turn round and it would all be over. But the whole beach was reverberating in the sun and pressing against me from behind. I took a few steps towards the spring. The Arab didn't move. Even now he was still some distance away. Perhaps because of the shadows on his face, he seemed to be laughing. I waited. The sun was beginning to burn my cheeks and I felt drops of sweat gathering in my eyebrows. It was the same sun as on the day of mother's funeral and again it was my forehead that was hurting me most and all the veins were throbbing at once beneath the skin. And because I couldn't stand this burning feeling any longer, I moved forward. I knew it was stupid and I wouldn't get out of the sun with one step. But I took a step, just one step forward. And this time, without sitting up, the Arab drew his knife and held it out towards me in the sun. The light leapt up off the steel and it was like a long, flashing sword lunging at my forehead. At the same time all the sweat that had gathered in my eyebrows suddenly ran down over my eyelids, covering them with a dense layer of warm moisture. My eyes were blinded by this veil of salty tears. All I could feel were the cymbals the sun was clashing against my forehead and, indistinctly, the dazzling spear still leaping up off the knife in front of me. It was like a red-hot blade gnawing at my eyelashes and gouging out my stinging eyes. That was when everything shook. The sea swept ashore a great breath of fire. The sky seemed to be splitting from end to end and raining down sheets of flame. My whole being went tense and I tightened my grip on the gun. The trigger gave, I felt the underside of the polished butt and it was there, in that sharp but deafening noise, that it all started. I shook off the sweat and the sun. I realized that I'd destroyed the balance of the day and the perfect silence of this beach where I'd been happy. And I fired four more times at a lifeless body and the bullets sank in without leaving a mark. And it was like giving four sharp knocks at the door of unhappiness.

PART TWO

I

Immediately after my arrest I was questioned several times. But it was only a matter of finding out who I was, which didn't take long. The first time, at the police station, nobody seemed very interested in my case. A week later though, the examining magistrate eyed me with curiosity. But to start with he simply asked me my name and address, my occupation and my date and place of birth. Then he wanted to know if I'd chosen a lawyer. I confessed that I hadn't and inquired as to whether it was absolutely necessary to have one. 'Why do you ask?' he said. I replied that I thought my case was very simple. He smiled and said, 'That's your opinion. But this is the law. If you don't choose a lawyer yourself, we'll appoint one for you automatically.' I thought it most convenient that the legal system should take care of such details. I told him so. He agreed and said it showed how well the law worked.

At first I didn't take him seriously. I was shown into a curtained room, there was just one lamp on his desk which was shining on the chair where he made me sit while he himself remained in the shadow. I'd read similar descriptions in books before and it all seemed like a game. After our conversation though, I looked at him and saw a tall, fine-featured man with deep-set blue eyes, a long grey moustache and a mass of almost white hair. I found him very reasonable and on the whole quite pleasant, in spite of a few nervous twitches he had about the mouth. On my way out I was even going to shake his hand, but I remembered just in time that I'd killed a man.

The next day a lawyer came to see me at the prison. He was short and stout, quite young, with his hair carefully greased back. In spite of the heat (I was in my shirt-sleeves), he was wearing a dark suit, a wing collar and a peculiar tie with broad black and white stripes. He put the briefcase which he had under his arm down on my bed, introduced himself and told me that he'd studied my file. My case was tricky, but he was confident of success, provided I had faith in him. I thanked him and he said, 'Let's get straight on with it.'

He sat down on the bed and explained that some investigations had been made into my private life. It had been discovered that my mother had died recently in a home. Enquiries had then been made at Marengo, and the magistrates had learned that I'd 'displayed a lack of emotion' on the day of mother's funeral. 'You will understand,' my lawyer said, 'that I feel rather embarrassed at having to ask you this. But it matters a great deal. And the prosecution will have a strong case if I can't find anything to reply.' He wanted me to help him. He asked me if I'd felt any grief on that day. This question really surprised me and I thought how embarrassed I'd have been if I'd had to ask it. I replied though that I'd rather got out of the habit of analysing myself and that I found it difficult to answer his question. I probably loved mother quite a lot, but that didn't mean

anything. To a certain extent all normal people sometimes wished their loved ones were dead. Here the lawyer interrupted me, looking very flustered. He made me
promise not to say that at the hearing, or in front of the
examining magistrate. But I explained to him that by
nature my physical needs often distorted my feelings.
On the day of mother's funeral I was very tired and
sleepy. So I wasn't fully aware of what was going on.
The only thing I could say for certain was that I'd rather
mother hadn't died. But my lawyer didn't seemed
pleased. He said, 'That's not enough.'

He thought for a moment. Then he asked me if he
could say that I'd controlled my natural feelings that day.
I said, 'No, because it's not true.' He looked at me in a
peculiar way, as if he found me slightly disgusting. He
told me almost spitefully that whatever happened the
warden and staff of the home would be called as witnesses and that this 'could make things very unpleasant
for me'. I pointed out to him that none of this had
anything to do with my case, but he merely replied that
I had obviously never had anything to do with the law.

He left, looking angry. I'd have liked to have kept
him back and explained to him that I wanted to be
friends with him, not so that he'd defend me better, but,
so to speak, in a natural way. The main thing was,
I could tell that I made him feel uncomfortable. He
didn't understand me and he rather held it against me.
I wanted to assure him that I was just like everyone
else, exactly like everyone else. But it was all really a bit
pointless and I couldn't be bothered.

Soon after that, I was taken to see the examining
magistrate again. It was two o'clock in the afternoon

and this time there was only a net curtain to soften the light which was flooding into his office. It was very hot. He made me sit down and very politely informed me that, 'due to unforeseen circumstances', my lawyer had been unable to come. But I was entitled not to answer his questions and to wait until my lawyer could assist me. I said I could answer for myself. He pressed a button on the table. A young clerk came and sat down right behind me.

We both sat back in our chairs. The examination began. He told me first of all that people described me as being taciturn and withdrawn and he wanted to know what I thought of that. I answered, 'It's just that I never have much to say. So I keep quiet.' He smiled as before, remarked that that was the best reason and added, 'Anyway, it doesn't matter at all.' He stopped talking and looked at me, then sat up rather suddenly and said very quickly, 'What interests me is you.' I didn't quite understand what he meant by that and I didn't say anything. 'There are certain things,' he added, 'that puzzle me in what you did. I'm sure you'll help me to understand them.' I told him that it was all very simple. He urged me to go over the day again. I went over what I'd already told him about: Raymond, the beach, the swim, the fight, the beach again, the little spring, the sun and the five shots. After each sentence he'd say, 'Fine, fine.' When I came to the outstretched body, he nodded and said, 'Good.' But I was tired of repeating the same story over and over again and I felt as if I'd never talked so much in all my life.

After a short silence, he stood up and told me that he wanted to help me, that I interested him and that with

God's help he would do something for me. But first, he wanted to ask me a few more questions. In the same breath, he asked me if I loved mother. I said, 'Yes, like everyone else,' and the clerk, who until now had been tapping away regularly at his typewriter, must have hit the wrong key, because he got in a muddle and had to go back. Still without any apparent logic, the magistrate then asked me if I'd fired all five shots at once. I thought it over and specified that I'd only fired once to start with and then, a few seconds later, the other four shots. 'Why did you pause between the first and the second shot?' he said. Once again I saw the red beach in front of me and felt the burning sun on my forehead. But this time I didn't answer. Throughout the silence which followed, the magistrate looked flustered. He sat down, ran his fingers through his hair, put his elbows on his desk and leaned slightly towards me with a strange expression on his face. 'Why, why did you fire at a dead body?' Once again I didn't know what to answer. The magistrate wiped his hands across his forehead and repeated his question in a slightly broken voice, 'Why? You must tell me. Why?' I still didn't say anything.

Suddenly he stood up, strode over to a far corner of his office and opened a drawer in a filing cabinet. He took out a silver crucifix and came back towards me brandishing it. And in an altogether different, almost trembling voice, he exclaimed, 'Do you know who this is?' I said, 'Yes, naturally.' Then he spoke very quickly and passionately, telling me that he believed in God, that he was convinced that no man was so guilty that God wouldn't pardon him, but that he must first repent and so become like a child whose soul is empty and ready to embrace everything. He was leaning right across the table, waving his crucifix almost directly over me. To tell the truth, I hadn't followed his argument at all well, firstly because I was hot and his office was full of huge flies which kept landing on my face, and also because he frightened me a bit. I realized at the same time that this was ridiculous because, after all, I was the criminal. But he carried on. I vaguely understood that as far as he was concerned there was only one part of my confession that didn't make sense, the fact that I'd paused before firing my second shot. The rest was all right, but this he just couldn't understand.

I was about to tell him that he was wrong to insist on this last point: it didn't really matter that much. But he interrupted me and pleaded with me one last time, drawing himself up to his full height and asking me if I believed in God. I said no. He sat down indignantly. He told me that it was impossible, that all men believed in God, even those who wouldn't face up to Him. That was his belief, and if he should ever doubt it, his life would become meaningless. 'Do you want my life to be meaningless?' he cried. As far as I was concerned, it had nothing to do with me and I told him so. But across the table, he was already thrusting the crucifix under my nose and exclaiming quite unreasonably, 'I am a Christian. I ask Him to forgive your sins. How can you not believe that He suffered for your sake?' I noticed that he was calling me by my first name, but I'd had enough. It was getting hotter and hotter. As I always do when I want to get rid of someone I'm not really listening to, I gave the impression that I was agreeing with him. To my surprise he was exultant. 'You see, you see,' he was saying, 'you do believe and you will put your trust in Him, won't you?' I obviously said no again. He sank back into his chair.

He looked very tired. For a moment he said nothing while the typewriter, which had followed the entire conversation, caught up with the last few sentences. Then he looked at me intently and rather sadly. He murmured, 'I have never seen a soul as hardened as yours. The criminals who have come to me before have always wept at the sight of this symbol of suffering.' I was about to reply that that was precisely because they were criminals. But I realized that I was like them too. It was an idea I just couldn't get used to. Then the magistrate stood up, as if to indicate that the examination was over. Only he asked me in the same rather weary manner whether I regretted what I'd done. I thought it over and said that, rather than true regret, I felt a kind of annoyance. I had the impression that he didn't understand me. But on that occasion that was as far as things went.

From then on I often went to see the examining magistrate. Only I was accompanied by my lawyer every time. I would simply be asked to clarify certain details of my previous statements. Or else the magistrate would discuss the charges with my lawyer. But actually they never took any notice of me on these occasions. Anyway, the tone of the examinations gradually changed. It seemed as if the magistrate had lost interest in me and had somehow classified my case. He didn't talk to me about God any more and I never saw him again in such a frenzy as on that first day. The result was that our discussions became more friendly. A few questions, a short conversation with my lawyer and the examinations would be over. My case was taking its course, to use the magistrate's own phrase. And sometimes, when the conversation was of a general nature, I would be included too. I began to breathe again. No one was unkind to me on these occasions. Everything was so natural, so well organized and so calmly acted out that I had the ridiculous impression of 'being one of the family'. And by the end of the eleven months which this investigation lasted, I must say I was almost surprised that I'd ever enjoyed anything other than those rare moments when the magistrate would escort me to the door of his study, slap me on the shoulder and say in a friendly voice, 'That's all for today, Mr Antichrist.' I would then be put back in the hands of the police.

2

There are some things I've never liked talking about. When I went to prison, I realized after a few days that I wouldn't like talking about this part of my life.

Later on, I didn't see any point in being so reluctant any more. In actual fact I wasn't actually in prison the first few days: I was vaguely waiting for something to happen. It was only after Marie's first and only visit that it all started. From the day I got her letter (telling me that they wouldn't let her come any more because she wasn't my wife), from that day on, I felt that my cell was my home and that my life was at a standstill. When I was first arrested, I was put in a room with several other prisoners, most of them Arabs. They laughed when they saw me. Then they asked me what I'd done. I told them that I'd killed an Arab and there was silence. But a few minutes later it began to get dark. They told me how to lay out the mat I had to sleep on. One end of it could be rolled up to make a bolster. All night I had bugs crawling over my face. A few days later I was confined to a cell by myself where I slept on a wooden bench. I had a toilet bucket and a tin basin. The prison was right at the top of the town and, through a tiny window, I could just see the sea. One day when I was clinging to the bars, with my face straining towards the light, a

warder came in and told me that I had a visitor.
I thought it must be Marie. It was.

To get to the visiting room I went down a long corridor, then down some stairs, and finally along another
corridor. I entered a very large room lit by a huge bay-
window. Two rows of bars ran the length of the room,
dividing it into three sections. Between the two rows of
bars was a gap of eight or ten yards which separated the
visitors from the prisoners. I noticed Marie standing
opposite me with her striped dress and her suntanned
face. On my side there were about ten prisoners, mostly
Arabs. Marie was surrounded by Moorish women and
standing between two visitors: a small, tight-lipped old
lady, dressed in black and a large, bare-headed lady who
was talking in a very loud voice and waving her arms
about. Because of the distance between the bars, both
visitors and prisoners had to raise their voices. When
I entered the room, the noise echoing off the huge, bare
walls and the harsh light pouring down out of the sky
and reflecting off the windows made me feel rather
dizzy. My cell was much quieter and darker. It took me
a few seconds to adjust. And yet I ended up seeing every
face clearly and distinctly in the bright light. I noticed
that there was a warder sitting at the far end of the space
between the two rows of bars. Most of the Arab
prisoners and their families had crouched down opposite each other. They weren't shouting. In spite of the
din, they were managing to make themselves heard by
talking in very low voices. Their muffled murmuring,
coming from lower down, formed a kind of continuo
for the conversations going backwards and forwards
above their heads. I took all this in very quickly as

I walked towards Marie. Already pressed up against the bars, she was smiling at me as hard as she could. I thought she looked very beautiful, but I didn't know how to tell her.

'Well?' she said in a very loud voice. 'Well, here I am.' 'Are you all right, have you got everything you want?' 'Yes, everything.'

We stopped talking and Marie went on smiling. The fat woman was yelling at the man next to me, a tall, blond, honest-looking chap who must have been her husband. They were in the middle of a conversation.

'Jeanne wouldn't take him,' she was shouting at the top of her voice. 'Yes, yes,' the man kept saying. 'I told her you'd take him back when you got out, but she wouldn't take him.'

Marie shouted across in turn that Raymond wished me well and I said, 'Thanks.' But my voice was drowned by the man next to me asking if he was 'all right'. His wife laughed and said he'd 'never been better'. The prisoner on my left, a small man with delicate hands, wasn't saying anything. I noticed that he was standing opposite the little old lady and that they were gazing intently at each other. But I didn't have time to watch them for very long because Marie shouted to me that I must keep hoping. I said, 'Yes.' At the same time I was looking at her and I wanted to squeeze her shoulders through her dress. I wanted to feel the soft material and I didn't quite know what else I was supposed to keep hoping for. But that must have been what Marie meant because she was still smiling. All I could see was the flash of her teeth and the little creases round her eyes. She shouted again, 'You'll get out and we'll get married!'

I answered, 'You think so?' but mainly to keep the conversation going. Then very quickly and still in a very loud voice she said yes, I'd be let off and we'd go swimming again. But the other woman was yelling across in her turn to say that she'd left a hamper in the clerk's office. She was enumerating all the things she'd put in it. He must check them all because they cost a lot of money. The man on the other side of me and his mother were still gazing at each other. The murmuring of the Arabs continued down below. Outside the light suddenly seemed to swell up against the bay-window.

I was feeling rather ill and I'd have liked to leave. I found the noise quite painful. But on the other hand, I wanted to make the most of having Marie there. I don't know how much time went by. Marie told me about her work and she never stopped smiling. The murmuring and the shouting and talking crossed backwards and forwards. The only oasis of silence was just next to me where the young man and the little old lady were gazing at each other. One by one the Arabs were taken away. Almost everyone stopped talking as soon as the first one went out. The little old lady stepped up to the bars and, at the same moment, a warder beckoned to her son. He said, 'Goodbye, mother,' and she put her hand through the bars to give him a long, slow little wave.

She went out as another man came in, hat in hand, and took her place. A prisoner was brought in and they began an animated conversation, but in low voices, because by now the room was silent again. They came to fetch the man on my right and his wife said to him, without lowering her voice as if she hadn't noticed that she didn't need to shout any more, 'Look after yourself and take care.' Then it was my turn. Marie blew me a kiss. I looked round before disappearing. She was standing quite still, with her face squashed up against the bars, and wearing that same strained, disjointed smile.

It was soon after that that she wrote to me. And it was from that point on that the things I've never liked talking about began. But after all, I mustn't exaggerate and it was easier for me than for others. When I was first imprisoned, though, the worst thing was that I kept thinking like a free man. For instance, I'd suddenly want to be on a beach and to be able to walk down to the sea. When I imagined the sound of the first little waves under the soles of my feet, the feel of the water on my body and the freedom it would give me, I'd suddenly realize how closed in I was by my prison walls. But that only lasted a few months. After that, I thought like a prisoner. I'd look forward to my daily walk in the courtyard or to my lawyer's visits. And I managed quite well the rest of the time. I often thought in those days that even if I'd been made to live in a hollow tree trunk, with nothing to do but look up at the bit of sky overhead, I'd gradually have got used to it. I'd have looked forward to seeing birds fly past or clouds run together just as here I looked forward to seeing my lawyer's curious ties and just as, in another world, I used to wait for Saturdays to embrace Marie's body. And come to think of it, I wasn't in a hollow tree. There were others unhappier than I was. Anyway it was an idea of mother's and she often used to repeat it, that you ended up getting used to everything.

Besides, I didn't usually take things as far as that. The first few months were bad. But the very fact that I had to make an effort helped me through them. For instance, I had a tormenting desire for a woman. That was only natural, I was a young man. I never thought specifically of Marie. But I'd so often be thinking about a woman, about women in general, about all the ones I'd known and all the occasions when I'd loved them, that my cell would fill with faces, the embodiments of my desires. In one sense, it unsettled me. But in another, it killed time. I'd ended up making friends with the chief warder who used to come round at meal times with the kitchen boy. He was the one who first talked to me about women. He told me that it was the first thing all the others complained about. I told him that I was like them and that I thought we were treated unfairly. 'Yes,' he said, 'but that's precisely why you're put in prison.' 'What do you mean, that's why?' 'Well, of course. Freedom, that's why. You're deprived of your freedom.' I'd never thought of that. I agreed. 'That's true,' I said, 'otherwise it wouldn't be punishment.' 'Right, you understand things, you do. The others don't. But they end up doing it by themselves.' The warder left after that.

Another thing was cigarettes. When I went into prison, they took away my belt, my shoe-laces, my tie and everything I had in my pockets, particularly my cigarettes. As soon as I got my cell, I asked for them back. But they told me that it wasn't allowed. The first few days were really bad. It was possibly this that shook me up the most. I used to break bits of wood off my bed-plank and suck them. I'd feel permanently sick all day long. I couldn't understand why I was being deprived of something that didn't do anyone any harm. Later on I realized that it was all part of the punishment. But by that time I'd got used to not smoking, so for me it was no longer a punishment.

Apart from these few annoyances, I wasn't too unhappy. The main problem, once again, was killing time. I ended up not being bored at all as soon as I learnt how to remember things. Sometimes I'd start thinking about my room and, in my imagination, I'd set off from one corner and walk round making a mental note of everything I saw on the way. At first it didn't take very long. But every time I did it, it took a bit longer. Because I'd remember every piece of furniture, and on every piece of furniture, every object and, on every object, every detail, every mark, crack or chip, and then even the colour or the grain of the wood. At the same time, I'd try not to lose track of my inventory, to enumerate everything. So that, by the end of a few weeks, I could spend hours doing nothing but listing the things in my room. And the more I thought about it the more things I dug out of my memory that I hadn't noticed before or that I'd forgotten about. I realized then that a man who'd only lived for a day could easily live for a hundred years in a prison. He'd have enough memories not to get bored. In a way, that was a good thing.

Another thing was sleeping. At first I didn't sleep well at night and I didn't sleep at all during the day. Gradually my nights got better and I managed to sleep during the day as well. In fact, during the last few months I was sleeping sixteen to eighteen hours a day. So that left me six hours to kill with my meals, my bodily functions, my memories and the story of the Czechoslovakian.

Between my mattress and my bed-plank, I'd actually found an old scrap of newspaper which had gone all yellow and transparent and was almost stuck to the material. It was a small news story. The beginning was missing, but it must have taken place in Czechoslovakia. A man had left some Czech village to go and make his fortune. Twenty-five years later he'd come back rich, with a wife and child. His mother and his sister were running a hotel in his native village. In order to surprise them, he'd left his wife and child at another hotel and gone to see his mother who hadn't recognized him when he'd walked in. Just for fun, he'd decided to book a room. He'd shown them his money. During the night his mother and his sister had clubbed him to death with a hammer to steal his money, and then thrown his body into the river. The next morning, the wife had come along and without realizing revealed the traveller's identity. The mother had hanged herself. The sister had thrown herself down a well. I must have read this story thousands of times. On the one hand, it was improbable. On the other, it was quite natural. Anyway, I decided that the traveller had deserved it really and that you should never play around.

So what with my sleeping for hours, remembering things, reading my news story and watching the changes of light and darkness, the time passed. I'd read somewhere that you ended up losing track of time in prison. But it hadn't meant much to me. I hadn't understood how days could be both long and short at the same time. Long to live through I suppose, but so distended that they ended up flowing into one another. They lost their names. The words yesterday and tomorrow were the only ones that still meant something to me.

When one day the warder told me that I'd been there five months, I believed it but I didn't understand it. For me it was for ever the same day that I was spinning out in my cell and the same task that I was pursuing. That day, after the warder had left, I looked at myself in my tin plate. My reflection seemed to stay serious even when I tried to smile at it. I shook it up and down in front of me. I smiled and it still looked sad and severe. It was the end of the day, the part I don't like talking about, the nameless part, when evening noises would rise up from every floor of the prison in a cortège of silence. I went up to the skylight and, in the fading light, I had another look at my reflection. It was still serious, and what was surprising about that when at that point I was serious too? But at the same moment, and for the first time in several months, I clearly heard the sound of my own voice. I recognized it as the one that had been ringing in my ears for days on end and I realized that all that time I'd been talking to myself. I then remembered what the nurse said at mother's funeral. No, there was no way out and no one can imagine what the evenings in prisons are like.

3

I must say that in fact summer very soon came round again. I knew that as soon as it began to get hot something new was going to happen to me. My case was down for the last session of the court of assizes and the session was due to end in June. The proceedings opened with blazing sunshine outside. My lawyer had assured me that they wouldn't last more than two or three days. 'Besides,' he'd added, 'the court won't want to waste any time because yours isn't the most important case in the session. There's a parricide coming on immediately afterwards.'

At half past seven in the morning they came to fetch me and the prison van took me to the Law Courts. The two policemen took me into a small room which smelt of shade. We sat down and waited by a door through which we could hear people talking and shouting, chairs scraping and a whole commotion which reminded me of one of those local festivals where, after the concert, they clear the room for dancing. The policemen told me that we had to wait for the court to convene and one of them offered me a cigarette which I refused. He asked me soon afterwards if I was 'nervous'. I said no. In fact, in a way it would be interesting to watch a trial. I'd never had the chance to see one before. 'Yes,' the other policeman said, 'but it ends up being boring.'

After a short while a little bell rang in the room. They then took off my handcuffs. They opened the door and led me into the dock. The room was full to bursting. In spite of the blinds, the sun was filtering through in places and the air was already stifling. They'd left the windows shut. I sat down with the policemen on either side of me. It was at that point that I noticed a row of faces in front of me. They were all looking at me: I realized that they were the jury. But I couldn't make any distinctions between them. I just had one impression: I was in a tram and all these anonymous passengers on the opposite seat were scrutinizing the new arrival to find his peculiarities. I know it was a silly idea since it wasn't peculiarities they were looking for here, but criminality. There's not much difference though and anyway that was the idea that came to me.

I was feeling a bit dizzy too with all these people in this stuffy room. I looked at the public again and I couldn't pick out a single face. I think at first I hadn't quite realized that all these people were crowding in to see me. Usually no one took any notice of me. I had to make an effort to understand that I was the cause of all this excitement. I said to the policeman, 'What a lot of people!' He replied that it was because of the papers and he pointed to a group standing by a table under the jury-box. He said, 'That's them.' I asked, 'Who?' and he repeated, 'The papers.' He knew one of the journalists who noticed him at that point and came towards us. He was an elderly and pleasant-looking man, with a rather twisted grin on his face. He shook hands very warmly with the policeman. I noticed at that point that everyone was meeting and welcoming everyone else and chatting away, as if this were some sort of club where people are happy to find themselves in a familiar world. That was how I explained the peculiar impression I had of being out of place, a bit like an intruder. And yet the journalist turned to me and smiled. He told me that he hoped everything would go well for me. I thanked him and he added, 'You know, we've blown your case up a bit. The summer's the silly season for the papers. And there was only your story and the one on the parricide that were worth doing.' After that he pointed towards the group he'd just come from at a little fellow with huge, black-rimmed spectacles who looked like an overweight weasel. He told me that he was the special correspondent of one of the Paris papers. 'He didn't actually come because of you. But since he's got to cover the parricide trial, they asked him to send a report on your case as well.' I nearly thanked him again. But I thought it would sound ridiculous. He gave me a friendly little wave and left us. We waited another few minutes.

My lawyer arrived, in a gown, surrounded by lots of other colleagues. He went over to the journalists and shook some hands. They joked and laughed and seemed completely at ease, until the bell rang in the court. Everyone went back to his seat. My lawyer came up to me, shook hands and advised me to reply briefly to any questions I might be asked, never to take the initiative and to rely on him to do the rest.

To my left I heard the sound of a chair being pulled back and I saw a tall, thin man, dressed in red and wearing a pince-nez, carefully folding his gown about him as he sat down. This was the prosecutor. An usher asked everyone to rise. At the same moment two huge fans started whirring round. Three judges, two in black, the third in red, came in carrying files and walked briskly up onto the platform which dominated the room. The man in the red gown sat down on the chair in the middle, placed his cap in front of him, wiped his little bald head with a handkerchief and announced that the court was in session.

The journalists already had their pens poised. They were all wearing the same indifferent and rather sardonic expression. And yet one of them, a much younger man in grey flannels and a blue tie, had left his pen lying in front of him and was looking at me. All I could see in his rather lop-sided face were his two very bright eyes, which were examining me carefully, without betraying any definable emotion. And I had the peculiar impression of being watched by myself. It may have been for that reason, and also because I was unfamiliar with all the procedures, that I didn't quite follow everything that happened after that, the drawing of lots by the jury, the questions put by the presiding judge to the lawyer, the prosecutor and the jury (each time, their heads would all turn at once towards the bench), a hurried reading of the indictment, during which I recognized names of people and places, and some more questions to my lawyer.

But the judge said he was going to move on to the calling of witnesses. The usher read out some names which caught my attention. Standing up one by one amidst what had previously been a shapeless mass of people, only to disappear again through a side door, I saw the warden and the caretaker from the home, old Thomas Pérez, Raymond, Masson, Salamano and Marie, who gave me an anxious little wave. I was still feeling surprised that I hadn't noticed them before, when the last name was called and Céleste stood up. I recognized the little woman from the restaurant sitting next to him with her jacket and her precise and purposeful manner. She was staring at me intently. But I didn't have time to think because the judge started speaking. He said that the formal proceedings were about to begin and that he didn't think he need remind the public to stay quiet. According to him, he was there to direct the proceedings impartially and to judge the case objectively. The verdict returned by the jury would be accepted in a spirit of justice and, whatever happened, he would have the court cleared if there was the slightest disturbance.

It was getting hotter and I could see people in the court fanning themselves with newspapers, which made a continuous little rustling sound. At a signal from the presiding judge, the usher brought in three straw fans which the three judges started using immediately.

My examination began at once. The presiding judge questioned me calmly and even, I thought, with a hint of friendliness. Once again I was asked to give my personal particulars, and although it irritated me, I realized that it was really quite natural, because there would be nothing worse than trying the wrong man. Then the judge started recounting what I'd done again, turning to me every couple of sentences to ask, 'Is that correct?' Each time, I answered, 'Yes, Your Honour,' following my lawyer's instructions. It took a long time because the judge went into minute detail in his account. All this time the journalists were writing away. I was conscious of being watched by the youngest of them and by the little robot-woman. Everyone on the tram was turned towards the judge, who coughed, leafed through a file and turned to me, still fanning himself.

He told me that he now had to touch upon certain matters which might seem foreign to my case, but which could in fact be highly relevant to it. I realized that he was going to talk about mother again and at the same time I could feel how much it annoyed me. He asked me why I'd sent mother to a home. I replied that it was because I didn't have enough money to have her looked after by a nurse. He asked me whether it had been a personal sacrifice for me and I replied that neither mother nor I expected anything more of each other, or in fact of anyone else, and that we'd both got used to our new lives. The judge then said that he didn't want to press the point and asked the prosecutor if he could think of any other questions to ask me.

The prosecutor had his back half turned to me and, without looking at me, he announced that with the judge's permission he'd like to know whether I'd gone back to the spring alone with the intention of killing the Arab. 'No,' I said. 'In that case, why was he armed and why return to precisely that spot?' I said it was by chance. And the prosecutor remarked in a malicious tone, 'That will be all for the present.' After that things were a bit confused, at least for me. But after a certain amount of conferring, the judge announced that the hearing was adjourned and would resume in the after-noon when the witnesses would be heard.

I didn't have time to think. I was taken out, put into the van and taken to the prison where I had something to eat. After a very short time, just long enough for me to realize that I was tired, they came back to fetch me; it all started again and I found myself in the same room, confronted by the same faces. Only it was much hotter and as if by a miracle each of the jurymen, the prosecutor, my lawyer and some of the journalists had also been provided with straw fans. The young journalist and the little woman were still there. But they weren't fanning themselves, they were just watching me as before in silence.

I wiped the sweat from my face and only vaguely remembered where I was and what I was doing there when I heard them call the warden of the home. He was asked whether mother used to complain about me and he said yes but that his inmates had rather a habit of complaining about their relatives. The judge asked him to specify whether she used to reproach me for having sent her to a home and the warden again said yes. But this time he didn't add anything. To another question he replied that he'd been surprised by my calmness on the day of the funeral. He was asked what he meant by calmness. The warden then looked down at his boots and said that I hadn't wanted to see mother, I hadn't cried once and I'd left straight after the funeral without paying my respects at her grave. And another thing had surprised him: one of the undertaker's men had told him that I didn't know how old mother was. There was a moment's silence and the judge asked him whether he had in fact been referring to me. The warden didn't understand the question, so the judge told him, 'It is the law.' Then he asked the Public Prosecutor whether he had any questions to put to the witness and the prosecutor exclaimed, 'Oh! no, that's quite sufficient,' in such a resounding voice and with such a triumphant glance in my direction that, for the first time in years, I stupidly felt like crying because I could tell how much all these people hated me.

After asking the jury and my lawyer whether they had any questions, the judge heard the caretaker's evidence. He too had to go through the same ceremony as all the others. When he stepped up, the caretaker glanced at me and then looked away. He answered the questions that were put to him. He said that I hadn't wanted to see mother, that I'd smoked, I'd slept and I'd had some white coffee. And I felt something stirring up the whole room; for the first time I realized that I was guilty. The caretaker was asked to repeat the story of the white coffee and the cigarette. The Public Prosecutor looked at me with an ironic gleam in his eye. At that point my lawyer asked the caretaker if he hadn't had a cigarette too. But the prosecutor protested violently against this question: 'Who is the criminal in this court and what is the meaning of casting aspersions on the witnesses for the prosecution in an attempt to detract from what is nothing less than damning evidence!' In spite of all this, the judge asked the caretaker to answer the question. The old man looked embarrassed and said, 'I know it was wrong. But I didn't dare refuse when the gentleman offered me a cigarette.' Finally I was asked if I had anything to add. 'Nothing,' I answered, 'except that the witness is right. It's true I offered him a cigarette.' The caretaker then gave me a rather surprised look as if he were somehow grateful. He hesitated and then said that it was he who had offered me the white coffee. My lawyer was exultant and announced in a loud voice that the jury would take note. But the prosecutor's voice boomed out over our heads and he said, 'Yes, the gentlemen of the jury will take note. And they will conclude that a stranger may offer a cup of coffee, but that a son must refuse it beside the body of the one who brought him into the world.' The caretaker went back to his seat.

When it came to Thomas Pérez, an usher had to help him over to the witness box. Pérez said that he'd really been a friend of my mother's and had only seen me once, and that was on the day of the funeral. He was asked how I'd behaved that day and he answered, 'Well, you see, I was really very upset. So I didn't notice anything. I was too upset to notice things. Because it was extremely upsetting for me. In fact I even fainted. So I didn't really notice the gentleman at all.' The Public Prosecutor asked him whether at least he'd noticed me cry. Pérez answered no. This time it was the prosecutor's turn to say, 'The gentlemen of the jury will take note.' But my lawyer lost his temper. He asked Pérez in what seemed to me an exaggerated tone of voice whether he'd noticed me 'not crying'. Pérez said, 'No.' The public laughed. And my lawyer rolled back one of his sleeves and announced peremptorily, 'Here we have the epitome of this trial. Everything is true and yet nothing is true!' The prosecutor's face was impassive and he was busy stabbing a pencil into the headings on his files.

After a five-minute adjournment during which my lawyer told me that everything was going well, we heard Céleste who was called by the defence. The defence meant me. Céleste was revolving a Panama hat in his hands and every now and then he'd throw a glance in my direction. He was wearing the new suit he sometimes used to put on on Sundays to come to the races with me. But I don't think he'd been able to get his collar on because he only had a brass stud holding his shirt together. He was asked whether I was one of his customers and he said, 'Yes, but a friend as well'; and what he thought of me and he replied that I was a man of the world; and what he understood by that and he announced that everyone knew what that meant; and whether he'd noticed that I was at all withdrawn and he simply remarked that I only spoke when I had something to say. The Public Prosecutor asked him whether I paid my board regularly. Céleste laughed and said, 'Things like that were just details between him and me.' Then he was asked what he thought of my crime. At that he placed his hands on the edge of the box and you could see that he'd prepared something. He said, 'I think it was a mishap. A mishap, everyone knows what that is. You can't guard against that. So there you are! I think it was a mishap.' He was going to go on, but the judge told him that that would be all and thanked him. Céleste was left rather dumbfounded. But he announced that he wanted to say something else. He was asked to be brief. He again repeated that it was a mishap. And the judge said, 'Yes, all right. But we are here to judge such mishaps. Thank you.' And as if all his knowledge and all his goodwill could avail him no

further, Céleste turned towards me. I thought I could
see his eyes glistening and his lips trembling. He seemed
to be asking me what more he could do. I didn't say
anything, I didn't even move, but it was the first time in
my life that I'd ever wanted to kiss a man. The judge
again instructed him to stand down. Céleste went back
to his seat among the public. He sat there throughout
the rest of the hearing, leaning slightly forwards, with
his elbows on his knees and the Panama hat in his hands,
listening to every word that was said. Marie came in.
She was wearing a hat and she still looked beautiful. But
I preferred her with her hair loose. From where I was
sitting I could just make out the slight swell of her
breasts and the familiar little pout of her lower lip. She
seemed very nervous. Straight away she was asked how
long she'd known me. She mentioned the time when
she used to work with us. The judge wanted to know
what our relationship was. She said she was my girl-
friend. To another question she replied that it was true
that she was to marry me. The prosecutor who was
leafing through a file asked her bluntly when our liaison
had begun. She mentioned the date. The prosecutor
remarked indifferently that it appeared to be the day
after mother's death. Then in a slightly ironic tone he
said that he didn't wish to dwell on such a delicate matter and that he fully understood Marie's scruples, but
(and here his voice suddenly became harder) that his
duty obliged him to rise above the level of proprieties.
He therefore asked Marie to describe the day on which
I'd had intercourse with her. Marie didn't want to, but
when the prosecutor insisted, she said how we'd swum
and been to the pictures and then gone back to my

place. The Public Prosecutor said that as a result of the statements made by Marie before the examining magistrate, he'd looked at the programmes for that day. He added that Marie herself would tell the court what film was showing. In an almost toneless voice, Marie indeed stated that it was a Fernandel film. There was complete silence in the court by the time she'd finished. The prosecutor then rose, looking very grave, and in a voice which I thought sounded truly emotional, and with a finger pointed in my direction, he slowly pronounced, 'Gentlemen of the jury, on the day after the death of his mother, this man was swimming in the sea, entering into an irregular liaison and laughing at a Fernandel film. I have nothing more to say to you.' He sat down, still amid silence. But all of a sudden Marie burst into tears and said it wasn't like that, there was something else and she was being made to say the opposite of what she thought, she knew me and I hadn't done anything wrong. But at a signal from the judge, the usher took her away and the hearing continued.

After that people hardly listened to Masson who announced that I was an honest chap, 'and what's more, a decent chap'. People hardly listened to Salamano either when he recalled how I'd been kind to his dog and when he replied to a question about me and my mother by saying that I'd run out of things to say to her and that was why I'd sent her to a home. 'You have to understand,' Salamano kept saying, 'you have to understand.' But no one seemed to understand. He was taken away.

Then it was Raymond's turn, as the last witness. Raymond gave me a little wave and immediately said that

I was innocent. But the judge announced that he wasn't being asked for value judgments, but for facts. He requested him to wait until he was questioned before speaking. He was asked to specify his relations with the victim. Raymond took this opportunity to say that he was the one that the victim hated because he'd beaten up his sister. The judge asked him nevertheless whether the victim didn't have reason to hate me. Raymond said that it was quite by chance that I happened to be at the beach. The prosecutor then asked him how it was that the letter which lay behind this intrigue had been written by me. Raymond replied that it was by chance. The prosecutor retorted that chance already had a number of misdemeanours on its conscience in this affair. He wanted to know if it was by chance that I hadn't intervened when Raymond had beaten up his mistress, by chance that I'd acted as a witness at the police station, and also by chance that the statements I'd made on that occasion had proved to be so thoroughly accommodating. Finally he asked Raymond what his means of livelihood were, and when Raymond replied that he was a 'warehouseman', the prosecutor announced to the jury that it was common knowledge that the witness earned a living as a procurer. I was his friend and accomplice. In fact the whole affair was of the most sordid description and what rendered it all the more iniquitous was the fact that they were dealing with an immoral monster. Raymond wanted to stand up for himself and my lawyer protested, but they were told that they must let the prosecutor finish. He said, 'I have little to add. Was he your friend?' he asked Raymond. 'Yes,' Raymond said, 'he was my mate.' The Public Prosecutor then asked me the same question. I met Raymond's eye and he didn't look away. I answered, 'Yes.' The prosecutor then turned to the jury and announced, 'Not only did this man indulge in the most shameful debauchery on the day after his mother's death, but he needlessly killed a man in order to resolve an intrigue of unconscionable immorality.'

He then sat down. But my lawyer was out of patience and, raising his arms so high that his sleeves fell back to reveal the folds of his starched shirt, he exclaimed, 'But after all, is he being accused of burying his mother or of killing a man?' The public laughed. But the prosecutor rose to his feet again, wrapped his gown about him and announced that only someone as naïve as the honourable counsel for the defence could fail to appreciate that between two such actions there existed a profound, tragic and vital relationship. 'Yes,' he exclaimed vehemently, 'I accuse this man of burying his mother like a heartless criminal.' This pronouncement seemed to have a considerable effect on the public. My lawyer shrugged his shoulders and wiped the sweat from his brow. But he looked shaken and I realized that things weren't going well for me.

The hearing was adjourned. For a few brief moments, as I left the Law Courts on my way to the van, I recognized the familiar smells and colours of a summer evening. In the darkness of my mobile prison I rediscovered one by one, as if rising from the depths of my fatigue, all the familiar sounds of a town that I loved and of a certain time of day when I sometimes used to feel happy. The cries of the newspaper sellers in the languid evening air, the last few birds in the square, the shouts of the sandwich sellers, the moaning of the trams high in the winding streets of the town and the murmuring of the sky before darkness spills over onto the port, all these sounds marked out an invisible route which I knew so well before going into prison. Yes, this was the time of day when, long ago, I used to feel happy. What always awaited me then was a night of easy, dreamless sleep. And yet something had changed, for with the prospect of the coming day, it was to my cell that I returned. As if a familiar journey under a summer sky could as easily end in prison as in innocent sleep.

4

Even when you're in the dock, it's always interesting to hear people talking about you. I must say, during the prosecutor's and my lawyer's speeches, a great deal was said about me, possibly even more about me than about my crime. Was there so much difference, anyway, between the two speeches? The lawyer raised his arms and pleaded guilty, but with mitigation. The prosecutor held out his hands and proclaimed my guilt, but without mitigation. There was one thing though that vaguely bothered me. In spite of all my worries, I'd occasionally feel tempted to intervene and my lawyer would always tell me, 'Keep quiet, it's better for you.' In a way, they seemed to be conducting the case independently of me. Things were happening without me even intervening. My fate was being decided without anyone asking my opinion. From time to time I'd feel like interrupting everyone and saying, 'But all the same, who's the accused? It's important being the accused. And I've got something to say!' But when I thought about it, I didn't really have anything to say. Besides, I must admit that the pleasure you get from having people listening to you doesn't last very long. For example, I very soon got bored with the prosecutor's speech. It was only isolated fragments, occasional gestures or lengthy tirades which caught my attention or aroused my interest.

The basis of his argument, if I understood correctly, was that my crime was premeditated. At least, that was what he tried to demonstrate. As he himself said, 'I shall prove it to you, gentlemen, and I shall prove it in two ways. With the blinding evidence of the facts to begin with and then by exposing the dark workings of this criminal soul.' He summarized the facts as from mother's death. We were reminded of my insensitivity, of my ignorance when asked how old mother was, of my swim the next day, with a girl, of the cinema, of Fernandel and finally of my return home with Marie. It took me a while to understand him at that point, because he kept saying 'his mistress', and to me she was Marie. After that he came to the business with Raymond. His way of looking at things certainly didn't lack clarity. What he said was quite plausible. I'd written the letter in collusion with Raymond as a bait for his mistress in order to subject her to ill-treatment by a man 'of doubtful morality'. I'd provoked Raymond's adversaries on the beach. Raymond had been wounded. I'd asked him for his gun. I'd gone back with the intention of using it. I'd shot the Arab as I'd planned. I'd waited. And 'to make sure I'd done the job properly', I'd fired four more shots, deliberately and at point-blank range and with some kind of forethought.

'So there you are, gentlemen,' the Public Prosecutor said, 'I have retraced for you the series of events which led this man to kill, in full consciousness of his actions. I emphasize this point,' he said. 'For this is no ordinary murder, a thoughtless act which you might consider extenuated by circumstances. This man, gentlemen, this man is intelligent. You have heard him, have you not? He knows how to answer. He knows the value of words. And no one can say that he acted without realizing what he was doing.'

I· was listening and I could hear that I was being judged intelligent. But I couldn't understand how the qualities of an ordinary man could be used as damning evidence of guilt. At least, that was the thing that struck me and I didn't listen to the prosecutor any more until at one point I heard him say, 'Has he even expressed any regrets? Never, gentlemen. Not once in front of the examining magistrate did he show any emotion with regard to his abominable crime.' At that point he turned towards me, pointed his finger at me and went on showering me with accusations without me really understanding why. Of course, I couldn't help admitting that he was right. I didn't much regret what I'd done. But I was surprised that he was so furious about it. I'd have liked to have explained to him in a friendly way, almost affectionately, that I'd never really been able to regret anything. I was always preoccupied by what was about to happen, today or tomorrow. But naturally, in the position I'd been put into I couldn't talk to anyone like that. I had no right to be affectionate or to show any goodwill. And I tried to listen again because the prosecutor started talking about my soul.

He said he'd peered into it and found nothing, gentlemen of the jury. He said the truth was that I didn't have one, a soul, and that I had no access to any humanity nor to any of the moral principles which protect the human heart. 'Of course,' he added, 'we can hardly reproach him for this. We can hardly complain that he lacks something he was never able to acquire. But here in this court the wholly negative ethic of tolerance must give way to the stricter but loftier ethic of justice. Especially when we encounter a man whose heart is so empty that it forms a chasm which threatens to engulf society.' That was when he started talking about my attitude towards mother. He repeated what he'd said in his opening speech. But he went on for much longer than when he was talking about my crime, so long in fact that in the end I was only conscious of the heat of the morning. That is until the prosecutor stopped and after a moment's silence, continued in a very deep and very earnest voice, 'Tomorrow, gentlemen, this same court will judge the most abominable of all crimes: the murder of a father.' According to him, the mind recoiled at the mere thought of such an atrocity. He ventured to hope that human justice would be unflinching in its condemnation. But he wasn't afraid to say that though this crime filled him with horror, he felt no less horror at my insensitivity. Again according to him, any man who was morally responsible for his mother's death thereby cut himself off from the society of men to no lesser extent than one who raised a murderous hand against the author of his days. In any case, the former paved the way for the latter, one act somehow heralded and legitimized the other. 'I am convinced, gentlemen,' he added, raising his voice, 'that you will not think it rash of me to suggest that the man who is sitting here in the dock is also guilty of the murder which this court is to judge tomorrow. He must be punished accordingly.' Here the prosecutor wiped his face which was glistening with sweat. He concluded by saying that his duty was a painful one, but that he would fulfil it resolutely. He announced that I had no place in a society whose most fundamental rules I ignored, nor could I make an appeal to the heart when I knew nothing of the most basic human reactions. 'I ask you for this man's head, and I do so with an easy mind,' he said. 'For though in the course of my long career I have often had occasion to demand capital punishment, never before have I felt this onerous task so fully compensated and counterbalanced, not to say enlightened by a sense of urgent and sacred duty as well as by the horror which I feel at the sight of a man in whom I see nothing but a monster.'

When the prosecutor sat down again, there was quite a long silence. I was so hot and so surprised that I felt dizzy. The judge coughed slightly and in a very low voice asked me if I had anything to add. I stood up and since I felt like talking, I said, rather haphazardly in fact, that I hadn't intended to kill the Arab. The judge replied that this was a positive statement, that so far he hadn't quite grasped my system of defence and that before hearing my lawyer he would be happy to have me specify the motives which had inspired my crime. Mixing up my words a bit and realizing that I sounded ridiculous, I said quickly that it was because of the sun. Some people laughed. My lawyer shrugged his shoulders and immediately afterwards he was asked to speak. But he announced that it was late and that he would need several hours, and he asked for an adjournment until the afternoon. The judges agreed.

That afternoon the huge fans were still churning up the dense atmosphere in the courtroom and the jurymen were all waving their little coloured fans in the same direction. I thought my lawyer's speech was never going to end. At one point though I listened because he said, 'It's true that I killed a man.' Then he went on like that, saying 'I' every time he meant me. I was very surprised. I leant over to one of the policemen and asked him why this was. He told me to be quiet and a moment later added, 'Lawyers always do that.' It seemed to me that it was just another way of excluding me from the proceedings, reducing me to insignificance and, in a sense, substituting himself for me. But I think I was already a very long way from that courtroom. Besides, I thought my lawyer was ridiculous. He made a quick plea of provocation and then he too started talking about my soul. But he didn't seem to have nearly as much talent as the prosecutor. 'I too,' he said, 'have peered into this man's soul, but unlike my eminent colleague from the State Prosecutor's office, I did find something there and in fact I read it like an open book.' He'd read that I was an honest chap, a regular and tireless worker who was faithful to the company that employed him, popular with everyone and sympathetic to the misfortunes of others. To him I was a model son who had supported his mother for as long as he could. In the end I'd hoped that an old people's home would give the old lady the comforts which my limited means prevented me from providing for her. 'I am amazed, gentlemen,' he added, 'that such a fuss has been made of this home. For after all, if proof were needed of the importance and usefulness of these institutions, one need only say that it is the state itself which subsidises them.' The only thing was that he didn't talk about the funeral and I felt that this was an important omission in his speech. But what with all these long sentences and the endless days and hours that people had been talking about my soul, I just had the impression that I was drowning in some sort of colourless liquid.

In the end all I remember is that, echoing towards me from out in the street and crossing the vast expanse of chambers and courtrooms as my lawyer went on talking, came the sound of an ice seller's trumpet. I was assailed by memories of a life which was no longer mine, but in which I'd found my simplest and most lasting pleasures: the smells of summer, the part of town that I loved, the sky on certain evenings, Marie's dresses and the way she laughed. And the utter pointlessness of what I was doing here took me by the throat and all I wanted was to get it over with and to go back to my cell and sleep. I hardly even heard my lawyer exclaim finally that the jury would surely not send an honest worker to his death just because he forgot himself for a moment, and then appeal for extenuating circumstances since my surest punishment for this crime was the eternal remorse with which I was already stricken. The court was adjourned and the lawyer sat down, looking exhausted. But his colleagues came over to shake hands with him. I heard a 'magnificent, old chap'. One of them even called me to witness. 'Eh?' he said. I agreed, but it was hardly a sincere compliment, because I was too tired.

However, the sun was getting low outside and it wasn't so hot any more. From the few street noises that I could hear, I sensed the calm of evening. There we all were, waiting. And what we were all waiting for concerned no one but me. I looked round the room again. Everything was just as it had been on the first day. I met the eye of the journalist in the grey jacket and of the little robot-woman. That reminded me that I hadn't looked for Marie once during the whole trial. I hadn't forgotten her, only I'd been too busy. I saw her sitting between Céleste and Raymond. She gave me a little wave as if to say, 'At last,' and I saw a rather anxious smile on her face. But my heart felt locked and I couldn't even smile back.

The judges returned. The jury was very rapidly read a series of questions. I heard 'guilty of murder . . .', 'premeditation . . .', 'extenuating circumstances'. The jury went out and I was taken into the little room where I'd waited once already. My lawyer came to join me: he was very talkative and spoke to me in a more confident and friendly way than he'd ever done before. He thought that everything would be all right and that I'd get off with a few years of prison or hard labour. I asked him whether there was any chance of getting the sentence quashed if it was unfavourable. He said no. His tactics had been not to lodge any objections so as not to antagonize the jury. He explained that they didn't quash sentences just like that, for no reason. It seemed obvious and I accepted his argument. Looking at it coldly, it was completely natural. If the opposite were the case, there'd be far too much pointless paperwork. 'Anyway,' my lawyer told me, 'you can always appeal. But I'm convinced the outcome will be favourable.'

We waited a very long time, almost three quarters of an hour, I think. At the end of that time a bell rang. My lawyer left me, saying, 'The foreman of the jury is going to read out the verdict. You'll only be brought in for the passing of the sentence.' Some doors banged. People were running up and down stairs, but I couldn't tell how far away they were. Then I heard a muffled voice reading something out in the courtroom. When the bell rang again and the door to the dock opened, what greeted me was the silence that filled the room, the silence and that strange sensation I had when I discovered that the young journalist had looked away. I didn't look over at Marie. I didn't have time to because the judge told me in a peculiar way that I would be decapitated in a public square in the name of the French people. And I think I recognized the expression that I could see on every face. I'm quite sure it was one of respect. The policemen were very gentle with me. The lawyer placed his hand on my wrist. I'd stopped thinking altogether. But the judge asked me if I had anything to add. I thought it over. I said, 'No.' That was when they took me away.

5

For the third time, I've refused to see the chaplain. I've got nothing to say to him, I don't feel like talking and I'll be seeing him soon enough as it is. What interests me at the moment is trying to escape from the mechanism, trying to find if there's any way out of the inevitable. I've been moved to another cell. From this one, when I'm lying down, I can see the sky and nothing else. I spend all day watching its complexion darken as day turns to night. I lie here with my hands under my head and wait. I don't know how many times I've wondered whether there have ever been instances of condemned prisoners escaping from the implacable machinery, disappearing before the execution or breaking through the police cordon. I'd reproach myself every time for not having paid enough attention to stories of executions. You should always take an interest in these things. You never know what might happen. Like everyone else I'd read newspaper reports. But there must have been special books which I'd never been curious enough to refer to. That was where I might have found stories of people who'd escaped. I might have discovered that there'd been at least one occasion when the wheel had stopped, that amongst so much that was inexorable and premeditated, chance or luck had just once managed to change something. Once! In a way, I think that would have been enough. My heart would have done the rest. The papers often talked about a debt being owed to society. According to them, it had to be paid. But that hardly appeals to the imagination. The vital thing was that there be a chance of escaping, of breaking out of this implacable ritual, of making a mad dash for it which would admit every possible hope. Naturally, that hope was of being shot down at a street corner, in full flight, and by a bullet from nowhere. But when I really thought about it, there was nothing to permit me such a luxury, everything was set against it, and I was caught in the mechanism again.

Willing as I was, I just couldn't accept such an absolute certainty. Because after all, the actual sentence which had established it was ridiculously out of proportion with its unshakeable persistence ever since the moment when that sentence had been passed. The fact that the sentence had been read out at eight o'clock rather than at five o'clock, and the fact that it might have been completely different, and that it had been decided upon by men who change their underwear, and that it had been credited to so vague an entity as the French (or German, or Chinese) people, all these things really seemed to detract considerably from the seriousness of such a decision. And yet I had to admit that from the very second it was taken, its consequences became just as certain, just as serious, as the fact that I was lying there flat against that wall.

At times like this I remembered a story that mother used to tell me about my father. I never met him. Perhaps the only thing I really knew about the man was this story that mother used to tell me: he'd gone to watch a murderer being executed. He'd felt ill at the thought of going. He had though and when he'd got back he'd been sick half the morning. My father disgusted me a bit at the time. But now I understood, it was completely natural. I don't know how I hadn't realized before that nothing was more important than executions and that, in actual fact, they were the only thing a man could really be interested in! If I ever got out of this prison, I'd go and watch all the executions there were. But I think I was wrong even to consider the possibility. For at the thought of being a free man standing there early in the morning behind a police cordon, on the other side as it were, and of being one of the spectators who come and watch and can be sick afterwards, my heart would suddenly be poisoned by a great flood of joy. But it was irrational. I was wrong to let myself make these suppositions because the next second I'd feel so dreadfully cold that it would make me curl up inside my blanket. My teeth would be chattering uncontrollably.

But naturally, you can't always be rational. At other times, for example, I'd work out new legal policies. I'd reform the punishment system. I'd realized that the essential thing was to give the condemned man a chance. Even one in a thousand was quite enough to sort things out. For instance, I imagined that they could find some chemical compound for the patient to take (I thought of him as the patient) which would kill him nine times out of ten. He would know this, that was the condition. Because when I really thought about it and considered things calmly, I could see that what was wrong with the guillotine was that you had no chance at all, absolutely none. In fact it had been decided once and for all that the patient would die. It was a classified fact, a firmly fixed arrangement, a definite agreement which there was no question of going back on. In the unlikely event of something going wrong, they just started again. Consequently, the annoying thing was that the condemned man had to hope that the machine worked properly. I say this is what's wrong with the system. That's true in a way. But in another way, I had to admit that it also possessed the whole secret of good organization. After all, the condemned man was obliged to lend moral support. It was in his interest that everything should go off without a hitch.

I was also made to realize that up until then I'd had mistaken ideas about these things. I've always thought – I don't know why – that to get to the guillotine you had to climb onto a scaffold, up some steps. I think it was because of the 1789 Revolution, I mean because of everything I'd been shown or taught about these things. But one morning I remembered seeing a photograph which had appeared in the papers at the time of a famous execution. In actual fact, the machine stood flat on the ground, as ordinary as anything. And it was much narrower than I'd thought. It was funny that it hadn't occurred to me before. The machine in this picture had struck me because it looked so immaculate and gleaming, like a precision instrument. You always get exaggerated ideas of things you know nothing about. I was made to realize that on the contrary everything was quite simple: the machine is on the same level as the man who's walking towards it. He goes up to it just as you would go to meet another person. That was annoying too. Climbing up into the sky to mount the scaffold was something the imagination could hang on to. Whereas, once again, the mechanism demolished everything: they killed you discreetly and rather shame-facedly but extremely accurately.

There were two other things I was always thinking about: the dawn and my appeal. I'd try to be rational though and not think about them any more. I'd stretch out and look at the sky and force myself to take an interest in it. It would turn green and I'd know it was evening. I'd make another effort to divert my thoughts. I'd listen to my heart. I couldn't imagine that this noise which had been with me for so long could ever stop. I've never really had much imagination. And yet I'd try to envisage a particular moment when the beating of my heart would no longer be going on inside my head. But in vain. Either the dawn or my appeal would still be there. And I'd end up telling myself that the most rational thing was not to hold myself back.

They came at dawn, I knew that. In fact I spent every night just waiting for the dawn to come. I've never liked being surprised. When something's happening to me, I'd rather be around. That's why I ended up only sleeping for a bit during the day, while all through the night I waited patiently for the dawn to break above the skylight. The most difficult part was that in-between time when I knew they usually operated. Once it was past midnight, I'd be waiting, listening. Never before had my ears picked up so many noises or detected such tiny sounds. I must say though that in a way I was lucky throughout that period in that I never once heard foot-steps. Mother often used to say that you're never altogether unhappy. And lying there in my prison when the sky turned red and a new day slid into my cell, I'd agree with her. Because I could just as easily have heard footsteps and my heart could have burst. For even though the faintest rustle would send me flying to the door and even though, with my ear pressed to the wood, I'd wait there frantically until I could hear my own breathing and be terrified to find it so hoarse, like a dog's death-rattle, my heart wouldn't burst after all and I'd have gained another twenty-four hours.

All through the day there was my appeal. I think I made the most of that idea. I'd calculate my assets so as to get the best return on my thoughts. I'd always assume the worst: my appeal had been dismissed. 'Well, then I'll die.' Sooner than other people, obviously. But everybody knows that life isn't worth living. And when it came down to it, I wasn't unaware of the fact that it doesn't matter very much whether you die at thirty or at seventy since, in either case, other men and women will naturally go on living, for thousands of years even. Nothing was plainer, in fact. It was still only me who was dying, whether it was now or in twenty years' time. At that point the thing that would rather upset my reasoning was that I'd feel my heart give this terrifying leap at the thought of having another twenty years to live. But I just had to stifle it by imagining what I'd be thinking in twenty years' time when I'd have to face the same situation anyway. Given that you've got to die, it obviously doesn't matter exactly how or when. Therefore (and the difficult thing was not to lose track of all the reasoning which that 'therefore' implied), therefore, I had to accept that my appeal had been dismissed.

At that point, and only at that point, I'd as it were have the right, I'd so to speak give myself permission to consider the alternative hypothesis: I was pardoned. The annoying thing was that somehow I'd have to control that burning rush of blood which would make my eyes smart and my whole body delirious with joy. I'd have to do my best to restrain this outburst, to be rational about it. I'd have to remain calm even about this hypothesis, in order to make my resignation to the first one more plausible. When I'd managed it, I'd have gained an hour's respite. That was something anyway.

It was at one such moment that I refused yet again to see the chaplain. I was lying down and I could tell from a slight glow in the summer sky that evening was approaching. I'd just dismissed my appeal and I could feel the regular pulse of my blood circulating inside me. I had no need to see the chaplain. For the first time in ages I thought of Marie. She hadn't written to me for days on end. That evening I thought it over and I told myself that she'd probably got tired of being a condemned man's mistress. It also crossed my mind that she might have been ill or dead. It was in the natural order of things. And how would I have known when, now that we were physically separated, there was nothing left to keep us together or to remind us of each other. Anyway, from that point on, Marie's memory would have meant nothing to me. I wasn't interested in her any more if she was dead. I found that quite normal just as I could quite well understand that people would forget about me once I was dead. They had nothing more to do with me. I couldn't even say that this was hard to accept.

It was at that precise moment that the chaplain walked in. A slight shiver went through me when I saw him. He noticed it and told me not to be afraid. I replied that he usually came at a different time. He told me that it was just a friendly visit and had nothing to do with my appeal which he knew nothing about. He sat down on my bunk and invited me to sit next to him. I refused. All the same, I found him quite pleasant.

He sat there for a moment, with his forearms on his knees, looking down at his hands. They were slim and muscular and they looked like a pair of nimble animals. He rubbed them slowly together. Then he sat like that, still looking down, for so long that for a second I thought I'd forgotten he was there.

But suddenly he raised his head and looked me in the face. 'Why do you refuse to see me?' he said. I replied that I didn't believe in God. He wanted to know whether I was quite sure about that and I said I had no reason for asking myself that question: it didn't seem to matter. He then leant back against the wall, with his hands flat on his thighs. Almost as if he were talking to himself, he remarked that sometimes you think you're sure when really you're not. I didn't say anything. He looked at me and asked, 'What do you think?' I replied that it was possible. In any case, I may not have been sure what really interested me, but I was absolutely sure what didn't interest me. And what he was talking about was one of the very things that didn't interest me.

He looked away and, still without changing position, asked me if I weren't talking like that out of utter despair. I explained to him that I wasn't in despair. I was simply afraid, which was only natural. 'In that case, God would help you,' he said. 'Every man that I've known in your position has turned towards Him.' I remarked that that was up to them. It also proved that they could spare the time. As for me, I didn't want anyone to help me and time was the very thing I didn't have for taking an interest in what didn't interest me.

At that point he made an irritated gesture, but then he sat up and straightened the folds of his gown. When he'd finished, he spoke to me, addressing me as 'my friend': it wasn't because I was condemned to death that he was talking to me like that; in his opinion, we were all condemned to death. But I interrupted him by saying that it wasn't the same thing and that anyway, this could never be any consolation. 'Admittedly,' he agreed. 'But if you don't die now, you'll die later. And the same problem will arise. How are you going to face up to that terrifying ordeal?' I replied that I'd face up to it exactly as I was facing up to it now.

He stood up when I said that and looked me straight in the eye. It was a game I knew well. I often used to play it with Emmanuel or Céleste and generally they'd look away. The chaplain knew the game well too, I could tell immediately: his gaze never faltered. His voice didn't falter either when he said, 'Have you really no hope at all and do you live in the belief that you are to die outright?' 'Yes,' I said.

He then lowered his head and sat down again. He told me that he pitied me. He thought it was more than a man could bear. All I knew was that he was beginning to annoy me. I turned away as well and went and stood under the skylight. I was leaning my shoulder against the wall. Without really following what he was saying,

I heard him start asking me questions again. He was talking in an anxious and insistent voice. I realized that he was getting emotional and I listened more carefully.

He was expressing his certainty that my appeal would be allowed, but I was burdened with a sin from which I must free myself. According to him, human justice was nothing and divine justice was everything. I pointed out that it was the former which had condemned me. He replied that it hadn't washed away my sin for all that. I told him I didn't know what a sin was. I'd simply been told that I was guilty. I was guilty and I was paying for it and there was nothing more that could be asked of me. At that point he stood up again and I realized that in such a narrow cell, if he wanted to move, he didn't have much choice. He either had to stand up or sit down.

I was staring at the ground. He took a step towards me and stopped, as if he didn't dare come any closer. He was looking up at the sky through the bars. 'You're mistaken, my son,' he said, 'there is more that could be asked of you. And it may well be asked of you.' 'And what's that?' 'You could be asked to see.' 'To see what?'

The priest looked all around him and replied in a voice which suddenly sounded extremely weary, 'I know how the suffering oozes from these stones. I've never looked at them without a feeling of anguish. But deep in my heart I know that even the most wretched among you have looked at them and seen a divine face emerging from the darkness. It is that face which you are being asked to see.'

I woke up a bit. I told him that I'd been looking at these walls for months. There wasn't anything or any-one in the world I knew better. Maybe, a long time ago,

I had looked for a face in them. But that face was the colour of the sun and burning with desire: it was Marie's face. I'd looked for it in vain. Now it was all over. And in any case, I'd never seen anything emerging from any oozing stones.

The chaplain looked at me almost sadly. By now I had my back right up against the wall and my forehead was bathed in light. He said a few words which I didn't hear and then asked me very quickly if I'd let him kiss me. 'No,' I said. He turned and walked over to the wall and ran his hand slowly across it. 'Do you really love this earth as much as that?' he murmured. I didn't answer.

He stayed facing the wall for quite a long time. I found his presence tiresome and aggravating. I was about to tell him to go away and leave me alone when suddenly he had a sort of outburst and turned towards me exclaiming, 'No, I can't believe you. You must surely at some time have wished for another life.' I replied that naturally I had, but that it meant nothing more than wishing I was rich or could swim fast or had a better-shaped mouth. It was the same kind of thing. But he stopped me because he wanted to know how I imagined this other life. So I shouted at him, 'One which would remind me of this life,' and in the same breath I told him that I'd had enough. He started talking to me about God again, but I went up to him and made one last attempt to explain to him that I didn't have much time left. I didn't want to waste it on God. He tried to change the subject by asking me why I wasn't calling him 'father'. That irritated me and I told him that he wasn't my father: he was on the same side as the others.

'No, my son,' he said, placing his hand on my shoulder. 'I'm on your side. But you can't see that because your heart is blind. I shall pray for you.'

Then, for some reason, something exploded inside me. I started shouting at the top of my voice and I insulted him and told him not to pray for me. I'd grabbed him by the collar of his cassock. I was pouring everything out at him from the bottom of my heart in a paroxysm of joy and anger. He seemed so certain of everything, didn't he? And yet none of his certainties was worth one hair of a woman's head. He couldn't even be sure he was alive because he was living like a dead man. I might seem to be empty-handed. But I was sure of myself, sure of everything, surer than he was, sure of my life and sure of the death that was coming to me. Yes, that was all I had. But at least it was a truth which I had hold of just as it had hold of me. I'd been right, I was still right, I was always right. I'd lived in a certain way and I could just as well have lived in a different way. I'd done this and I hadn't done that. I hadn't done one thing whereas I had done another. So what? It was as if I'd been waiting all along for this very moment and for the early dawn when I'd be justified. Nothing, nothing mattered and I knew very well why. He too knew why. From the depths of my future, throughout the whole of this absurd life I'd been leading, I'd felt a vague breath drifting towards me across all the years that were still to come, and on its way this breath had evened out everything that was then being proposed to me in the equally unreal years I was living through. What did other people's deaths or a mother's love matter to me, what did his God or the lives people chose or the destinies they selected matter to me, when one and the same destiny was to select me and thousands of millions of other privileged people who, like him, called themselves my brothers. Didn't he understand? Everyone was privileged. There were only privileged people. The others too would be condemned one day. He too would be condemned. What did it matter if he was accused of murder and then executed for not crying at his mother's funeral? Salamano's dog was worth just as much as his wife. The little automatic woman was just as guilty as the Parisian woman Masson had married or as Marie who wanted me to marry her. What did it matter that Raymond was just as much my mate as Céleste who was worth more than him? What did it matter that Marie now had a new Meursault to kiss? Didn't he understand that he was condemned and that from the depths of my future . . . I was choking with all this shouting. But already the chaplain was being wrested from me and the warders were threatening me. He calmed them though and looked at me for a moment in silence. His eyes were full of tears. Then he turned away and disappeared.

Once he was gone, I felt calm again. I was exhausted and I threw myself onto my bunk. I think I must have fallen asleep because I woke up with stars shining on my face. Sounds of the countryside were wafting in. The night air was cooling my temples with the smell of earth and salt. The wondrous peace of this sleeping summer flooded into me. At that point, on the verge of daybreak, there was a scream of sirens. They were announcing a departure to a world towards which I would now be forever indifferent. For the first time in a very long time I thought of mother. I felt that I understood why at the end of her life she'd taken a 'fiancé' and why she'd pretended to start again. There at the home, where lives faded away, there too the evenings were a kind of melancholy truce. So close to death, mother must have felt liberated and ready to live her life again. No one, no one at all had any right to cry over her. And I too felt ready to live my life again. As if this great outburst of anger had purged all my ills, killed all my hopes, I looked up at the mass of signs and stars in the night sky and laid myself open for the first time to the benign indifference of the world. And finding it so much like myself, in fact so fraternal, I realized that I'd been happy, and that I was still happy. For the final consummation and for me to feel less lonely, my last wish was that there should be a crowd of spectators at my execution and that they should greet me with cries of hatred.

AFTERWORD

A long time ago, I summed up *The Outsider* in a sentence which I realize is extremely paradoxical: 'In our society any man who doesn't cry at his mother's funeral is liable to be condemned to death.' I simply meant that the hero of the book is condemned because he doesn't play the game. In this sense, he is an outsider to the society in which he lives, wandering on the fringe, on the outskirts of life, solitary and sensual. And for that reason, some readers have been tempted to regard him as a reject. But to get a more accurate picture of his character, or rather one which conforms more closely to his author's intentions, you must ask yourself in what way Meursault doesn't play the game. The answer is simple: he refuses to lie. Lying is not only saying what isn't true. It is also, in fact especially, saying more than is true and, in the case of the human heart, saying more than one feels. We all do it, every day, to make life simpler. But, contrary to appearances, Meursault doesn't want to make life simpler. He says what he is, he refuses to hide his feelings and society immediately feels threatened. For example, he is asked to say that he regrets his crime, in time-honoured fashion. He replies that he feels more annoyance about it than true regret. And it is this nuance that condemns him.

So for me Meursault is not a reject, but a poor and naked man, in love with a sun which leaves no shadows. Far from lacking all sensibility, he is driven by a tenacious and therefore profound passion, the passion for an absolute and for truth. This truth is as yet a negative one, a truth born of living and feeling, but without which no triumph over the self or over the world will ever be possible.

So one wouldn't be far wrong in seeing *The Outsider* as the story of a man who, without any heroic pretensions, agrees to die for the truth. I also once said, and again paradoxically, that I tried to make my character represent the only Christ that we deserve. It will be understood, after these explanations, that I said it without any intention of blasphemy but simply with the somewhat ironic affection that an artist has a right to feel towards the characters he has created.

Albert Camus,
8 January 1955

ABOUT THE INTRODUCER

PETER DUNWOODIE is Reader in French Literature at the University of London and the author of *A. Camus: 'L'Envers et l'Endroit'* and *'L'Exil et le Royaume'* (1985), *Une histoire ambivalente: Le dialogue Camus-Dostoïevski* (1996) and *Writing French Algeria* (1998). He has also written numerous articles on Camus, Louis-Ferdinand Céline and French Algerian fiction.

This book is set in BEMBO which was cut
by the punch-cutter Francesco Griffo
for the Venetian printer-publisher
Aldus Manutius in early 1495
and first used in a pamphlet
by a young scholar
named Pietro
Bembo.